The Young Engineers in Arizona; or, Laying Tracks on the Man-killer Quicksand

by H. Irving Hancock

CHAPTER I. THE MAN OF "CARD HONOR"

"I'll wager you ten dollars that my fly gets off the mirror before yours does."

"I'll take that bet, friend."

The dozen or so of waiting customers lounging in Abe Morris's barber shop looked up with signs of renewed life.

"I'll make it twenty," continued the first speaker.

"I follow you," assented the second speaker.

*Truly, if men must do so trivial a thing as squander their money on idle bets, here was a novel enough contest.

Each of the bettors sat in a chair, tucked up in white to the chin. Each was having his hair cut.

At the same moment a fly had lighted on each of the mirrors before the two customers.

The man who had offered the bet was a well known local character—Jim Duff by name, by occupation one of the meanest and most dishonorable gamblers who had ever disgraced Arizona by his presence.

There is an old tradition about "honest gamblers" and "players of square games." The man who has been much about the world soon learns to understand that the really honest and "square" gambler is a creature of the imagination. The gambler makes his living by his wits, and he who lives by anything so intangible speedily finds the road to cheating and trickery.

Jim Duff had been no exception. His reputation was such that he could find few men among the residents of this part of Arizona who would meet him at the gaming table. He plied his trade mostly among simple-minded tourists from the east—the class of men who are known in Arizona as "tenderfeet."

Rumor had it that Jim Duff, in addition to his many years of unblushing cheating for a living, had also shot and killed three men in the past on as many different occasions.

Yet he was a sleek, well-groomed fellow, tall and slim, and, in the matter of years, somewhere in his forties. Duff always dressed well—with a foundation of the late styles of the east, with something of the swagger of the plains added to his raiment.

"Stranger, you might as well hand me your money now," drawled Duff, after a few moments had passed. "It'll save time."

"Your fly hasn't hopped yet," retorted the second man, with the air and tone of one who could afford to lose thousands on such stupid bets.

The second man was of the kind on which Jim Duff fattened his purse. Clarence Farnsworth, about twenty-five years of age, was as verdant a "tenderfoot" as had lately graced Paloma, Arizona, with his presence.

Even the name of Clarence had moved so many men to laughter in this sweltering little desert town that Farnsworth had lately chopped his name to

"Clare." Yet this latter had proved even worse; it sounded too nearly like a girl's name.

So far as his financial condition went, Clarence had the look of one who possessed money to spend. He was well-dressed, lived at the Mansion House, often hired automobiles, entertained his friends lavishly, and was voted a good enough fellow, though a simpleton.

"My fly's growing skittish, stranger," smiled Jim Duff. "He's on the point of moving. You'd better whisper to your fly."

"I believe, friend," rejoined Clarence, "that my fly is taking nap. He appears to be sound asleep. You certainly picked the more healthy fly."

Jim Duff gave his barber an all but imperceptible nudge in one elbow. Though he gave no sign in return, that barber understood, and shifted his shears in a way that, even at distance, alarmed the fly on the mirror before Duff.

"Buzz-zz!" The fly in front of the gambler took wing and vanished toward the rear of the store.

Some of the Arizona men looking on smiled knowingly. They had realized from the start that young Farnsworth had stood no show of winning the stupid wager.

"You win," stated young Clarence, in a tone that betrayed no annoyance.

Drawing a roll of bills from his pocket, he fumbled until he found a twenty. This he passed to Duff, sitting in the next chair.

"You're not playing in luck to-day," smiled Duff gently, as he tucked away the money in one of his coat pockets. "You're a good sportsman, Farnsworth, at any rate."

"I flatter myself that I am," replied Clarence, blushing slightly.

Jim Duff continued calmly puffing at the cigar that rested between his teeth. They were handsome teeth, though, in some way, they made one think of the teeth of a vicious dog.

"Coming over to the hotel this afternoon?" continued Duff.

"I—I—" hesitated Clarence.

"Coming, did you say?" persisted Duff gently.

"I shall have to see my mail first. There may be letters—"

"Oh," nodded Duff, with just a trace of irony as the younger man again hesitated.

"Life is not all playtime for me, you know," Farnsworth continued, looking rather shame-faced. "I—er—have some business affairs attention at times."

"Oh, don't try to join me at the hotel this if you have more interesting matters in prospect," smiled the gambler.

Again Clarence flushed. He looked up to Jim Duff as a thorough "man of the world," and wanted to stand well in the gambler's good opinion. Clarence Farnsworth was, as yet, too green to know that, too often, the man who has seen much of the world has seen only its seamy and worthless side. Possibly Farnsworth was destined to learn this later on—after the gambler had coolly fleeced him.

"Before long," Farnsworth went on, changing the subject, "I must get out on the desert and take a look at the quicksand that the railroad folks are trying to cross."

"The railroad people will probably never cross that quicksand," remarked Jim Duff, the lids closing over his eyes for a moment.

"Oh, I don't know about that," continued Farnsworth argumentatively.

"I think I do," declared Jim Duff easily. "My belief, Farnsworth, is that the railroad people might dig up the whole of New Mexico, transport the dirt here and dump it on top of that quicksand, and still the quicksand would settle lower and lower and the tracks would still break up and disappear. There's no bottom to that quicksand."

"Of course you ought to know all about it, Duff," Clarence made haste to answer. "You've lived here for years, and you know all about this section of the country."

That didn't quite suit the gambler. What he sought to do was to raise an argument with the young man—who still had some money left.

"What makes you think, Farnsworth, that the railroad can win out with the desert and lay tracks across the quicksand? That's a bad quicksand, you know. It has been called the 'Man-killer.' Many a prospector or cow-puncher has lost his life in trying to get over that sand."

"The real Man-killer quicksand is a mile to the south of where the tracks go, isn't it?" asked Farnsworth.

"Yes; and the first party of railway surveyors who went over the line for their track thought they had dodged the Man-killer. Yet what they'll find, in the end, is that the Man-killer is a bad affair, and that it extends, under the earth, in many directions and for long distances. I am certain that railway tracks will never be laid over any part of the Man-killer."

"Perhaps not," assented Clarence meekly.

"What makes you think that the railroad can ever get across the Man-killer?" persisted Duff.

"Why, for one thing, the very hopeful report of the new engineers who have taken charge."

"Humph!" retorted Duff, as though that one word of contempt disposed of the matter.

"Reade and Hazelton are very good engineers, are they not?" inquired young Farnsworth.

"Humph! A pair of mere boys," sneered Jim Duff.

"Young fellows of about my age, you mean?" asked Farnsworth.

"Of your age?" repeated Duff, in a tone of wonder. "No! You're a man. Reade and Hazelton, as I've told you, are mere boys. They're not of age. They've never voted."

"Oh, I had no idea that they were as young as that," replied Clarence, much pleased at hearing himself styled a man. "But these young engineers come from one of the Colorado, railroads, don't they!"

"I wouldn't be surprised," nodded the gambler. "However, the Man-killer is no task for boys. It is a job for giants to put through, if the job ever can be finished."

"Then, if it's so difficult, why doesn't the road shift the track by two or three miles?" inquired Clarence.

"You certainly are a newcomer here," laughed Duff easily. "Why, my son, the railroad was chartered on condition that it run through certain towns. Paloma, here, is one of the towns. So the road has to come here."

"But couldn't the road shift, just after it leaves here?" insisted Clarence.

"Oh, certainly. Yet, if the road shifted enough to avoid any possibility of resting on the big Man-killer, then it would have to go through the range beyond here—would have to tunnel under the hills for a distance of three miles. That would cost millions of dollars. No, sir; the railroad will have to lay tracks across the Man-killer, or else it will have to stand a loss so great as to cripple the road."

"Excuse me, sir," interrupted a keen, brisk, breezy-looking man, who had entered the shop only a moment or two before. "There's a way that the railroad can get over the Man-killer."

"What is that?" asked Duff, eyeing the newcomer's reflected image in the mirror.

"The first thing to do," replied the stranger, "is to drop these boy engineers out of the game. These youngsters came down here four days ago, looked over the scene, and promised that they could get the tracks laid-safely—for about two hundred and fifty thousand dollars."

"Pooh!" jeered Duff, with a sidelong glance at young Farnsworth.

"Of course it is pooh!" laughed the stranger. "The thing can it be done for any such amount as that, and it is a crazy idea, to take the opinions of boys, anyway, on any such subject as that. Now, there's a Chicago firm of contractors, the Colthwaite Construction Company, which has proposed to take over the whole contract for laying tracks across the Man-killer. These boys figure on using dirt and then more dirt, and still more, until they've satisfied the appetite of the Man-killer, filled up the quicksand and laid a bed of solid earth on which the tracks will run safely for the next hundred years. The Colthwaite people have looked over the whole proposition. They know that it can't be done. The two hundred and fifty thousand dollars will be wasted, and then the Colthwaite Company will have to come in, after all, drive its pillars of steel and concrete, lay well-founded beds and get a basis that will hold the new earth above it. Then the track will be safe, and the people of this part of Arizona will have a railroad of which they can be proud. But these boys—these kids in railroad building—humph!"

"Humph!" agreed Jim Duff dryly.

The gambler using the mirror before him, continued to study keenly this stranger, even after the latter had ceased talking and had gone to one of the chairs to wait his turn.

"You're through, sir," announced the barber who had been trying to improve the gambler's appearance. "Thank you, sir. Next."

Clarence, wholly crushed by the weight of opinion, was not yet through with his barber. Duff, after lighting a fresh cigar, stepped over to where the newcomer was seated.

"Are you stopping at the Mansion House?" inquired the gambler.

"Yes," answered the stranger, looking up.

"So am I," nodded the gambler. "So I shall probably have the pleasure of meeting you again."

"Why, yes; I trust so," replied the stranger, after a quick, keen look at Duff. Undoubtedly this newcomer was accustomed to judging men quickly after seeing them.

"These boy engineers!" chucked Duff. "Humph!"

"Humph!" agreed the stranger.

At this moment two bronzed-looking, erect young men came tramping down the sidewalk together. Each looked the picture of health, of courage, of decision. Both wore the serviceable khaki now so common in surveying camps in warm climates. Below the knee the trousers were confined by leggings. Above the belt blue flannel shirts showed, yet these were of excellent fabric and looked trim indeed. To protect their heads and to shade their eyes as much as possible from the glare of Arizona desert sand, these young men wore sombreros of the type common in the Army.

"This looks like a good place, Harry," said the taller of the two young men. "Suppose we go inside."

They stepped into the barber shop together, nodding pleasantly to all inside. Then, hanging up their sombreros, they passed on to unoccupied chairs.

Just in the act of passing out, Jim Duff had stepped back to admit them.

"They're Reade and Hazelton, the very young engineers that the railroad has just put in charge of the Man-killer job," whispered one knowing citizen of Paloma. The news quickly spread about the barber shop.

Jim Duff already knew the boys by sight, since they were stopping at the Mansion House. He uttered an almost inaudible "humph!" then passed on outside.

Neither Tom Reade nor Harry Hazelton heard this exclamation, nor would they have paid any heed to it if they had.

Yes; the two young men were our friends of old, the young engineers. Our readers are wholly familiar with Tom and Harry as far back as their grammar school days in the good old town of Gridley. Tom and Harry were members of that famous sextet of schoolboy athletes known at home as Dick & Co. The exploits of Tom Reade and Harry Hazelton, as of Dick Prescott, Dave Darrin, Greg Holmes and Dan Dalzell, have been fully told, first in the "Grammar School Boys Series," and then in the "High School Boys Series."

After the close of the "High School Boys Series" the further adventures of Dick Prescott and Greg Holmes are told in the "West Point Series," while all that befell Dave Darrin and Dan Dalzell has already been found in the pages of the "Annapolis Series."

In the preceding volume of this series, "The Young Engineers in Colorado," our readers were made familiar with the real start in working life made by Tom

7

Reade and Harry Hazelton. Back in the old High School days Reade and Hazelton had been fitting themselves to become civil engineers. They began their real work in the east, and had made good in sterner work in the mountains in Colorado.

Our readers all know how Tom and Harry opened their careers in Colorado by becoming "cub engineers" with one of the field camps of the S. B. & L. railroad. Taken only on trial, they had rapidly made good, and had earned the confidence of the chief engineer in charge of the work. When, owing to the sudden illness of both the chief engineer and his principal assistant the road's work had been crippled, Tom and Harry had had the courage as well as the opportunity to take hold, assume the direction, and complete the building of the S. B. & L. within the time required by the road's charter.

Had the young engineers failed, the S. B. & L., under the terms granted by the state, might have been seized and sold at public auction. In that case, the larger, and rival road, the W. C. & A., stood ready to buy out the S. B. & L. and reap the profits that the latter road had planned to earn. Not only had the young engineers succeeded in overcoming all natural obstacles, but, in a series of wonderful adventures, they had defeated the plots of agents of the W. C. & A. From that time on Tom and Harry had been famous in Colorado railroad circles.

After the S. B. & L. had been finished and put in operation, Tom Reade had remained with the railroad for several months, still serving as chief engineer, with Harry Hazelton as his trusted and dependable assistant.

Now, at last, they had been lured away from the S. B. & L. by the offer of a new chance to overcome difficulties of the sort that all fighting engineers love to encounter. The Arizona, Gulf & New Mexico Railroad—more commonly known as the A., G. & N. M.—while laying its tracks in an attempt at record-beating, had come afoul of the problem of the quicksand, as already outlined. Three different sets of engineers had attempted the feat of filling up the quicksand, only to abandon it.

There was little doubt that the Colthwaite Construction Company, a contracting firm with years of successful experience, could have, "stopped" the quicksand, but this Chicago firm wanted far more money for the job than the railroad people felt they could afford to spend.

So, in a moment of doubt, and harassed by troubles, one of the directors of the A., G. & N. M. had remembered the names and the performances of Tom and Harry. This director of the Arizona road, being a friend of President Newnham, of the S. B. & L. road, had written the latter, asking whether the services of Tom and Harry could be secured. The reply had been in the affirmative, and Tom and Harry had speedily traveled down into Arizona. In the few days they had been at this little town of Paloma, they had gone thoroughly over the ground, they had studied the problem, and had expressed their opinion that the job could be put through creditably at a cost not exceeding a quarter of a million dollars.

"Go to it, then!" General Manager Curtis had replied. "You have our road's credit at your command, and we look to you to make good. You are both very young, but Newnham's word is quite good enough for us."

The day before this story opens this general manager had boarded one of the rough-looking construction trains and had gone back to the road's headquarters.

As they sat in the barber shop now Tom and Harry were quite unaware of the interested notice they were receiving. This was not surprising, for both were good, sane, wholesome American boys, with no more than the average share of conceit, and neither believed himself to be as much of a wonder as some experienced railroad men credited them with being.

"Stranger, excuse me, but you're Reade, aren't you?" inquired one of the men of Paloma who was present.

"Yes, sir," nodded Tom, looking up pleasantly from the weekly paper that he had been scanning.

"You're head of the new job on the Man-killer, aren't you?" questioned the same man. By this time every man in the barber shop was secretly watching the young engineers, a fact that was plain to Harry Hazelton, as he glanced up from a magazine.

"Yee, sir," Tom answered again. "In a way I'm at the head of it, but my friend, Hazelton, is really as much at the head as I am. We are partners, and we work together in everything."

"Do you think, Reade, that you're going to win out on the job?" inquired another man.

"Yes, sir," nodded Tom.

"You seem very confident about it," smiled another.

"It's just a way we have," Tom assented good-naturedly. "We always try to keep our nerve and our confidence with us."

"Yet you are really sure?"

"Oh! yes," Reade answered. "We have looked the quicksand over, and we feel sure that we see a way of stopping the Man-killer, and forcing it to sustain railroad ties and steel rails."

"How are you going; to go about it?" questioned still another interested citizen. These men of Paloma had good reason for being interested. When the iron road was finished, Paloma would be an intimate part of the now outside world. It was certain that Paloma real estate would rise to three or four times its present value.

"I know you'll excuse us," replied Tom, still speaking pleasantly, "if we don't go into precise details."

"Then you are going to make a secret of your plans?" inquired another barber-shop idler. His tone expressed merely curiosity; Arizona men are proverbially as polite as they are frank.

"We're somewhat secretive—yes, sir," Tom replied. "That is only because we regard the method we are going to use as being mainly the concern of the A., G. & N. M. No offense meant, sir, either."

"No offense taken," replied the late questioner.

Tom had already, within a few minutes, made an excellent impression on the majority of these Arizona men present.

As to the other newcomer, who had lately spoken so warmly of the Colthwaite Company, he was now silent, apparently greatly absorbed in a three-days-old newspaper that he had picked up. Yet he managed to cast more than one covert glance at the boys.

"I have heard both of you young men spoken of most warmly, as real engineers who are going to solve the problem of the Man-killer," declared Clarence Farnsworth, as, alighting from the barber's chair, he strolled past the pair.

"Thank you," nodded Tom, with all his usual simple good nature.

"If you make a successful job of it is will be a splendid thing for you in your professional careers," continued Farnsworth, rather aimlessly.

"Undoubtedly," nodded Harry.

The stranger who had held so much converse with Jim Duff was through with the barber at last. Though the day was scorchingly hot in this desert town, the stranger stepped along briskly until he had reached the hotel.

The Mansion House would scarcely have measured up to the hotel standards of large cities. Yet it was a very good hotel, indeed, for this part of Arizona, and the proprietor did all in his power for the comfort of his guests.

As the stranger ascended the steps to the broad porch he caught sight of Jim Duff, approaching the doorway from the inside.

"Oh, how do you do?" was Duff's greeting. "Hot, isn't it?"

"Very," nodded the stranger.

"I usually have my luncheon in my room, which is large and airy," continued Duff. "As I dislike to eat alone, I have ordered the table spread for two. I shall be very glad of your company, stranger, if you care to honor me."

"That is kind of you," nodded the other. "I shall accept with much pleasure, for I, too, like to eat in good company."

After a little more conversation the two ascended to Duff's room on the next floor. Certainly it was the largest and most comfortable guest room in the hotel, and was furnished in good taste. The main apartment was set as a gentlemen's lounging room, Duff's bedroom furniture being in a little room at the rear.

Hardly had Duff pressed the bell button before there came a tap at the door. One waiter brought in a table for two, with the napery. This he quickly arranged. As he turned toward the door two other waiters entered with dishes containing a dainty meal for a hot day.

"You may arrange everything and then leave us, John," directed Duff. Soon the two new acquaintances were alone together, the gambler serving the light meal with considerable grace.

"How long have you been with the Colthwaite Company?" asked Jim Duff presently.

"I didn't say that I had ever been with the Colthwaite Company," smiled the stranger.

"No," admitted the gambler; "but I took that much for granted."

Again the eyes of the two men met in an exchange of keen looks, Then the stranger laughed.

"Mr. Duff, I realize that it is a waste of time to try to conceal rather evident facts from you. I am Frederick Ransom, a special agent for the Colthwaite Company."

"You are down here to get the contract for filling up the Man-killer quicksand?" Duff continued, with an air of polite curiosity.

"The contract is not to be awarded," Ransom answered. "The A., G. & N. M. has decided to do the work itself, with the assistance of two young engineers who have been retained."

"Reade and Hazelton," nodded Jim Duff.

"Yes."

"They may fail—are almost sure to do so. Then, of course, Mr. Ransom, you will have a very excellent chance of securing the contract for the Colthwaite Company."

"Why, yes; if the young men do fail."

"Will you pardon a stranger's curiosity, Mr. Ransom? Have you laid your plans yet for the way in which the young men are to fail?"

From most strangers this direct questioning would have been offensive. Jim Duff, however, from long experience in fleecing greenhorns, had acquired a manner and way, of speaking that stood him in good stead.

After a moment's half-embarrassed silence Fred Ransom burst into a laugh that was wholly good-natured.

"Mr. Duff, You are unusually clever at reading other's motives," he replied.

"I went to school as a youngster, and learned how to read the pages of open books," the gambler confessed modestly. "So you have, as yet, no plan for compelling the young engineers to fail and quit at the Man-killer?"

This was such a direct, comprehensive question that Fred Ransom remained silent for some moments before he admitted:

"No; as yet I haven't been able to form a plan."

"Then engage me to help you," spoke Jim Duff slowly, coolly. "I know the country here, and the people. I know where to lay my finger on men who can be trusted to do unusual things. I shall come high, Mr. Ransom, but I am really worth the money. Talk it over with me, and convince me that your company will be sufficiently liberal in return for large favors."

"Oh, the Colthwaite Company would be liberal enough," protested Ransom, "and quick to hand out the cash, at that."

"I took that for granted," smiled Duff, showing his white teeth. "Your people, the Colthwaites, have always been accustomed to paying for favors that require unusual talent, some courage-and perhaps a persistency of the shooting kind."

Then the two rascals, who now thoroughly understood each other, fell to plotting. An hour later the outlook was dark, indeed, for the success of Tom Reade and Harry Hazelton.

CHAPTER II. DUFF ASSERTS HIS "RIGHTS"

"We've a hard afternoon ahead of us, Harry," remarked Tom Reade, as the engineer chums finished the noonday meal in the public dining room of the Mansion House.

"Pshaw! We'll have more real work to do after our material arrives," rejoined young Hazelton. "We're promised the material in four days. If we get it in a fortnight we will be lucky."

"That might be true on some railroads," smiled Tom. "But Mr. Ellsworth, the general manager of the A., G. & N. M., is a hustler, if I ever met one. When we wired to him what we needed, he wired back that enough of the material would be here within four days to keep us busy for some time. I believe Mr. Ellsworth never talks until he knows what he's talking about."

"Well, I hope you can find some work for the men to do this afternoon," murmured Harry, as the two young engineers rose from table. "Hawkins, our superintendent of construction, has about five hundred mechanics and laborers who will soon need work."

"Yes," agreed Tom. "The men took the jobs with the understanding that their pay would run on."

"The day's wages for five hundred workmen is a big item of loss when we're delayed," mused Hazelton.

"There's another consideration that's even worse than the loss," Tom went on in a low voice. "The pay train will be here this afternoon and the men will have a lot of money by evening. This town of Paloma is going to be wide open to-night in the effort to get the money away from our five hundred men."

"We can't stop that," sighed Harry. "We have no control over the way in which the workmen choose to spend their money."

"Want me to tell you a secret?" whispered Tom mysteriously.

"Yes, if it's an interesting one," smiled Harry.

"Very good, then. I know I can't actually interfere with the way the men spend their money. But I'm going to give them some earnest advice about avoiding fellows who would fleece them out of their wages."

"Go slowly, Tom!" warned Hazelton, opening his eyes rather wide. "Don't put yourself in bad with the men, or they may quit you in a body."

"Let them," retorted Tom, with one of his easy smiles. "If these men throw up their work General Manager Ellsworth will know where to find others for us. Few of our men are skilled workers. We can find substitutes for most of them anywhere that laborers can be found."

"But you've no right—"

"Of one thing you may be very sure, Harry. I'll take pains not to step over the line of my own rights, and not to step on the rights of the men who are working for us. What I mean to do is to offer them some very straight talk. I shall also warn them that we are quite ready to discharge any foolish fellows who may happen to go on sprees and unfit themselves for our work. I've one surprise to show you, Harry. Wait until Johnson, the paymaster, gets in. Then you'll see who else is with him."

"Are you gentlemen ready for your horses?" asked a stable boy, coming around to the front of the hotel.

"Yes," nodded Tom.

Two tough, lean, wiry desert ponies were brought around. Tom and Harry mounted, riding away at a slow trot at first.

From an upper window Fred Ransom looked down upon them, then called Duff to his side.

"There is your game, Duff," hinted the agent.

"They'll be easy to a man of my experience," laughed the gambler. "I've a clever scheme for starting trouble with them."

He whispered a few words in his companion's ears, at which Ransom laughed with apparent enjoyment.

"You're a keen one, Duff," grinned the agent from Chicago.

"I've seen enough of life," boasted the gambler quietly, "to be able to judge most people at first sight. You shall soon see whether I don't succeed in starting some hard feeling with Reade and Hazelton."

The nearer edge of the treacherous Man-killer was something more than two miles west of the town of Paloma. In the course of a quarter of an hour Tom and Harry drew rein near a portable wooden building that served as an office in the field.

Mr. Hawkins, a solid-looking, bearded man of fifty, with snapping eyes that contrasted with his drawling speech, stepped from the building.

"Hawkins," called Tom, as a Mexican boy led the horses away to the shade of a stable tent, "I see you have some men idle."

"Nine-tenths of 'em are idle," replied the superintendent of construction. "I warned you, Mr. Reade, that our gangs would soon eat up the little work that you left us. Out there, by the last cave-in you'll see that Foreman Payson, has about fifty men going. They'll be through within an hour."

"And the material, even if delivered within the promised time, is still two days away," remarked Reade. "I'll confess that I don't like to see the railroad lose so much through paying men for idle time."

"It can't be helped, sir," replied the superintendent. "Of course, if you like, you can set the laborers at work shoveling in more dirt at the points where the last slide of the quicksand occurred. But, then, shoveling dirt in, without the timbers and the hollow steel piles will do no good," continued Hawkins, with a shake of his head. "It would be worse than wasted work."

"I know all that," Tom admitted. "To tell you the truth, Mr. Hawkins, I wouldn't mind the men's idleness quite so much if it weren't that the pay train comes in this afternoon. An idle man, not over-nice about his habits, and with a lot of money in his pockets, is a source of danger. We're going to have five hundred such danger spots as soon as the men are paid off."

"Don't know that, sir!" demanded Superintendent Hawkins. "The town of Paloma is just dancing on sand-paper, it's so uneasy about getting its hand into the pile of more than thirty-eight thousand dollars that the pay train is going to bring in this afternoon."

"I know," nodded Tom rather gloomily. "I hate to see the men fleeced as they're likely to be fleeced to-night. Some of our men will be so badly done up that it will be a week before they get back to work—unless there is some way that we can stop the fleecing."

"There isn't any such way," declared Superintendent Hawkins, with an air of conviction.

13

"You've surely been around rough railroading camps enough to know that, Mr. Reade."

"I've seen a good deal of the life, Hawkins," Tom answered, "but of course I don't know it all."

"Yet you know that you can't hope to stop railroad jacks from spending their money in their own way. The saloons in Paloma will take in thousands of dollars from our lads to-night and all day to-morrow. The gamblers will swindle them out of a whole lot more. Day after to-morrow, Mr. Reade, you wouldn't be able to borrow twenty dollars from our whole force."

"It's a shame," burst from Tom indignantly, as the three turned to gaze westward across the desert. "These men work as hard as any toilers in the world. They receive good wages. Yet where do you find a railroad jack who, after years and years of toil on these burning deserts, has two or three hundred dollars of his own saved?"

Hawkins shrugged his shoulders.

"I know all about it," he responded, "and I grow angry every time I think about it. Yet how is one going to protect these, men against themselves?"

"I believe there's a way," spoke Tom confidently.

"I hope you can find it, then, Mr. Reade," retorted Hawkins skeptically.

"At any rate, I'm going to try."

"What are you going to do, Mr. Reade?" demanded the superintendent curiously.

"You'll be with me, won't you?" coaxed Tom.

"You'll stand with us, shoulder to shoulder."

"I certainly will, Mr. Reade!"

"And the foremen? You can depend upon them?"

"On every one of them," declared Hawkins promptly. "Even to the Mexican foreman, Mendoza. He's a greaser, but he's a brick, and a white man all the way through!"

"Call the foremen in, then—all except Payson, who is with his gang."

Tom and Harry stepped inside the office. Mr. Hawkins strolled away, but within ten minutes he was back again, followed by Foremen Bell, Rivers and Mendoza.

"Two wagons have driven up, east of here," announced Mr. Hawkins, as he entered the office building. "They've stopped a quarter of a mile below here and have dumped two tents. I think they're about to raise them."

Tom stepped hastily outside, glancing eastward, where they saw what the superintendent had described. One of the tents had just been raised, though the pitching of it had not yet been thoroughly done.

"What crowd is that?" Reade asked. "Who is at the head of it?"

"I see one man there—the only man in good clothes—who looks like Jim Duff," replied the superintendent, using his field glasses.

"The gambler?" asked Tom sharply.

"The same."

"He's pitching his tent on the railroad's dirt, isn't he!"

"Yes, sir."

14

"Come along. We'll have a look at that place."

A few minutes of brisk walking brought the young engineers, the superintendent and the three foremen to the spot.

Tent number one had been pitched. It was a circular tent, some forty feet in diameter. The second tent, only a little smaller, was now being hoisted.

"Who's in charge of this work?" asked Tom in his usual pleasant tone.

"My manager, Mr. Bemis—Dock Bemis," answered Jim Duff suavely, as he moved forward to meet the party. "Dock, come here. I want you to know Mr. Reade, the engineer in charge of this job."

Duff's manners were impudently easy and assured. The fellow known as Dock Bemis, an unprepossessing, shabbily dressed man of thirty-five, with a mean face and an ugly-looking eye, came forward.

"I'll take Mr. Bemis's acquaintance for granted," Tom continued, with an easy smile. "You own this outfit, don't you, Mr. Duff?"

"I've rented it, if you mean the tents, tables and chairs," assented the gambler. "I've a stock of liquors coming over as soon as I send one of the wagons back."

"What do you propose to do with all this?" Tom inquired.

"Why, of course, you see," smiled Duff, with all the suavity in the world, "as your boys are going to be paid off this afternoon they'll want to go somewhere to enjoy themselves. As the day is very hot I thought it would be showing good intentions if I brought an outfit over here. I'll have everything ready within an hour."

"So that you can get our men intoxicated and fleece them more easily?" asked Tom, with his best smile. "Is that the idea?"

Jim buff flushed angrily. Then his face became pale.

"It's a crude way you have of expressing it, Mr. Reade, if you Ill allow me to say so," the gambler answered, in a voice choked with anger. "I am going to offer your men a little amusement. It's what they need, and what they'll insist upon. Do you see? There's a small mob coming this way now."

Tom turned, discovering about a hundred railroad laborers coming down the road.

"Mr. Duff," asked the young chief engineer, "can you show any proof of your authority to erect tents on the railroad's land?"

"What other place around here, Mr. Reade, would be as convenient?" demanded the gambler.

"I repeat my question, sir! Have you any authority or warrant for erecting tents heie?"

"Do you mean, have I a permit from the railroad company?"

"You know very well what I mean, Duff."

Though Reade's tone was somewhat sharper, his smile was as genial as ever.

"I didn't imagine you'd have any objection to my coming here," the gambler replied evasively.

"Have you any authority to be on the railroad's land's?" persisted Tom Reade. "Yes or no?"

"No-o-o-o, I haven't, unless I can persuade you to see how reasonable it is that your men should be provided with enjoyment right at their own camp."

"Take the tents down, then, as quickly as you can accomplish it," directed Tom, though in a quiet voice.

"And—if I don't?" asked Duff, smiling dangerously and displaying his white, dog-like teeth.

"Then I shall direct one of the foremen to call a sufficient force, Mr. Duff, to take down your tents and remove them from railroad property. I am not seeking trouble with you, sir; I don't want trouble. But, as long as I remain in charge here no gambling or drinking places are going to be opened on the railroad's land."

"Mr. Reade," inquired the gambler, his smile fading, "do you object to giving me a word in private?"

"Not at all," Tom declared. "But it won't help your plans."

"I'd like just a word with you alone," coaxed the gambler.

Nodding, Reade stepped away with the gambler to a distance of a hundred feet or so from the rapidly increasing crowd.

"I expect to make a little money out of this tent outfit, of course," explained Jim Duff.

"I expect that you won't make a dollar out of it—on railway property," returned Reade steadily.

"I'm going to make a little money—not much," Duff went on. "Now, if I can make the whole deal with you, and if no one else is allowed to bother me, I can afford to pass you one hundred dollars a day for the tent privilege."

Before even expectant Tom realized what was happening, Duff had pressed a wad of paper money into his hand.

"What is this?" demanded Reade.

"Don't let everyone see it," warned the gambler. "You'll find two hundred dollars there, in bills. That's for the first two days of our tent privilege here."

"You contemptible hound!" exclaimed Tom angrily.

Whish! The tightly folded wad of bank notes left Tom's hand, landing squarely in Jim Duff Is face.

In an instant the gambler's face turned white. His hand flew back to a pocket in which he carried a pistol.

CHAPTER III. TOM MAKES A SPEECH ON GAMBLING

"Cut out the gun-play! That doesn't go here!" Tom uttered warningly.

One swift step forward, and one hand caught Jim Duff by the throat. With the other hand Tom caught Duff's right wrist and wrenched away the pistol that instantly appeared in the gambler's hand.

The weapon Tom threw on the ground, some feet away. Then, with eyes blazing with contempt, Tom Reade struck the gambler heavily across the face with the flat of his hand. Hard work had added to the young engineer's muscle of earlier days, and the gambler was staggered.

Another instant, and Superintendent Hawkins who, with Hazelton and the foremen, had run up to them, seized Duff roughly from behind, holding his arms pinioned.

Harry Hazelton picked up the revolver. Quickly opening it, he drew out the cartridges.

"Mr. Bell!" called Harry, and the foreman of that name hastened to him.

"Take this thing back to the office and break it up with a hammer," directed young Hazelton, as he passed the revolver to the foreman. The latter sped away on his errand.

"Let Duff go, Mr. Hawkins," directed Tom. "I'm not afraid of him. Duff, I wish to apologize to you for striking you in the face. I wouldn't allow any man to do that to me. But your action in reaching for a pistol was so childish—or cowardly, whichever you prefer to call it—that I admit I forgot myself for a moment. Now, you are not going to erect any tents for gambling or other unworthy purposes on the railroad's property. It's bad business to let you do anything of the sort. I trust that there will be no hard feeling between us."

"Hard feeling?" hissed Jim Duff, his wicked-looking face paler than ever. "Boy, you needn't try to crawl back into my good graces after the way you acted toward me!"

"I'm not trying to crawl into your esteem, or to get there by any other means," Tom answered quietly, though with a firmness that caused superintendent and foremen to feel a new respect for their young chief engineer. "At the same time, Duff, I don't believe in stirring up bad blood with anyone. You and I haven't the same way of regarding your line of business. That's the main difficulty. As I can't see your point of view, it would be hardly fair to expect you to understand my way of regarding what you wished to do here. Your tents will have to come down and be moved, but I have no personal feeling in the matter. How soon can you get your tents down?"

"They are not coming down, I tell you!" snarled the gambler.

"That's where you and I fail once more to agree," replied Tom steadily, looking the other straight in the eyes. "It's merely a question of whether you will take them down, or whether I shall set our own men to doing it."

Jim Duff had brought with him about a dozen men of his own. They were a somewhat picturesque-looking crowd, though not necessarily dangerous men. They were mostly men who had been hired to run the gaming tables under the canvas. A judge of men would have immediately classified them as inferior specimens of manhood.

So far these men had not offered to take any part in the dispute. Now Duff moved over to them quickly, muttering the words:

"Stand by me!"

As for Tom Reade, he was backed by five men, including his chum. Though none of Reade's force was armed, the young engineer knew that he could depend upon them.

Followed by his adherents, Duff took a few quick strides forward. This brought him face to face with Reade's labors, of whom now more than two hundred were present.

"Are you men or squaws?" called, Duff loudly. "I have brought the stuff over here for a merry night of it. This boy says you can't have your enjoyment. Are you going to let him rule you in that fashion, or are you going to throw him out of here?"

There came from the crowd a gradually increasing murmur of rage.

"Throw this boy out, if you're men!" Duff jeered. "Throw him out, I say, and send word to your railroad people to put a man here in his place."

The murmurs increased, especially from the Mexicans, for the Mexican peon, or laborer, is often a furious gambler who will stake even the shirt on his back.

Foreman Mendoza, who understood his own people, started forward, but Tom, with a signal, caused him to halt.

"Throw him out, I say!" yelled Duff shrilly. "Duff, I'm afraid you're making a fool of yourself," remarked Tom, stepping forward, smiling cheerfully.

Yet another murmur, now growing to a yell, rose from some of the men—a few of the men, too, who were not Mexicans, and a half-hearted rush was made in the young engineer's direction.

"Throw him out! Hustle the boy out!" Duff urged.

"Stop! Stop right in your tracks!" thundered Tom Reade, taking still another step toward the now angrier crowd. "Men, listen to me, and you'll get a proper understanding of this affair. Jim Duff wants me thrown out of here—"

"Yes! And out you'll go!" roared a voice from the rear of the crowd.

"That's a question that the next few minutes will settle," Tom rejoined, with a smile. "If Jim Duff wants me thrown out of here, why don't you men tell him to do it himself?"

The force of this suggestion, with the memory of what they had recently seen, struck home with many of the men. A shout of laughter went up, followed by yells of:

"That's right—dead right!"

"Sail in, Jim!"

"Throw him out, Jim! We'll see fair play!"

Tom made an ironical bow in the direction of the gambler.

"Have you men gone crazy!" yelled Jim Duff hoarsely.

"Have you lost your nerve, Jim?" bawled a lusty American laborer. "You want this boy, as you call him, thrown out, and we're waiting to see you do it. It you haven't the nerve to tackle the job, then you're not a man to give us orders!"

Tom's smiling good humor and his fair proposition had swung the balance of feeling against the gambler. Duff saw that he had lost ground.

"Boy," called a few voices, "if Duff won't throw you out, then you turn the tables and throw him out."

"It isn't necessary," laughed Tom. "After the tents are gone Duff won't have any desire to remain around here. Mr. Duff, I ask you for the last time, will you have your men take down the tents and remove them?"

"I won't!" snarled the gambler.

"Mr. Rivers!" called Tom.

"Yes, sir," replied the foreman, stepping forward.

"Mr. Rivers, take twenty-five laborers and bring the tents down at once. Be careful to see that no damage is done. As soon as they are down you will load them on the wagons."

"Yes, sir."

"On second thought, you had better take fifty men. See that the work is done as promptly as possible."

The Mexicans, who were in the majority, and nearly all of whom were wildly eager to gamble as soon as their money arrived, stirred uneasily. They might have interfered, but Foreman Mendoza ran among his countrymen, calling out to them vigorously in Spanish, and with so much emphasis that the men sullenly withdrew.

Foreman Rivers speedily had his fifty men, together, none of whom were Mexicans.

"Touch a single guy-rope at your peril!" warned Jim Duff menacingly, but big Superintendent Hawkins seized the gambler by the shoulders, gently, though, firmly, removing him from the vicinity of the tents.

All in a flash the work was done. Canvas and poles were loaded on to the wagons. Mr. Rivers's men had entered so thoroughly into the spirit of the thing that, they forced the drivers to start off, and the gambler's men to follow.

Goaded to the last ditch of desperation, Jim Duff now strode over to where Tom stood. No one opposed him, nor did Reade's smile fail.

"Boy, you've had your laugh, just now," announced the gambler, in his most threatening, tone. "It will be your last laugh."

"Oh, I hope not," drawled Tom.

"You will know more within twenty-four hours. You have treated me, with your own crowd about you, like a dog."

"You're wrong again," laughed Tom.. "Jim is fond of dogs. They are fine fellows."

"You may laugh as much as you want, just now," jeered Jim Duff. "You've made an enemy, and one of the worst in Arizona! I won't waste any more talk on you—except to warn you."

"Warn me? About what?" asked Tom curiously.

Instead of answering, Jim Duff turned on his heel, stalking off with a majesty that, somehow, looked sadly damaged.

"He has warned you," murmured Superintendent Hawkins in an undertone. "That is your hint that Duff will fight you to the death at the first opportunity."

"May it be long in coming!" uttered Tom devoutly.

Then, as he turned about and saw scores of laborers coming in his direction, Reade remembered what he wished to do.

"Mr. Hawkins," he continued, turning toward the superintendent, "I see that Mr. Payson's gang is coming in from work. As all our men are now idle, I wish you would direct the foremen to see that all hands assemble here. I have something to say to them."

Within ten minutes the five hundred laborers and mechanics had been gathered in a compact crowd. Now that the excitement of hustling the gambler off the scene had died away, many of the men were sorry that they had not made their disapproval plainer. Though Tom Reade plainly understood the mood of the men, he mounted a barrel, holding up both hands as a sign for silence.

"Now, men," he began, "you all know that the pay train is due here this afternoon. You are all eager to get your money—for what? It is a strange fact that gold is the carrion that draws all of the vultures. A few minutes ago you saw one of the vultures here, preparing to get his supposed share of your money away from you. Does Jim Duff care a hang about any of you? Do any of you care anything whatever for Jim Duff? Then why should you be so eager to get into one of his tents and let him take your money away from you?

"It is true that, once in a while, a solitary player gets a few dollars away from a gambler. Yet, in the end, the gambler has every dollar of the crowd that patronizes him. You men have been out in the hot sun for weeks, working hard to earn the money that the pay train is bringing you. Has Jim Duff done any work in the last few weeks? While you men have been toiling and sweating, what has Duff been doing? Hasn't he been going around wearing the clothes and the air of a gentleman, while you men have been giving all but your lives for your dollars, while you have been denied most of the comforts of living. Hasn't Duff been up at the Mansion House, living on the fat of the land and smiling to himself every time he thought of you men, who would be ready to hand him all of your money as soon as it came to you? Is the gambler, who grows fat on the toil of others, but never toils himself, any better than the vulture that feeds upon the animals killed by others? Isn't the gambler a parasite, pure and simple? On whose lifeblood does the gambler feed, unless it's on yours?"

Tom continued his harangue, becoming more and more intense, yet carrying his talk along in all simplicity, and with a directness that made scores of the workmen look sheepish.

"Whenever you find a man anywhere who professes to be working for your good, or for your amusement, and who gets all the benefit in the end, why don't you open your eyes to him?" Tom inquired presently. "Over in Paloma there are saloon keepers who are cleaning up their dives and opening new lots of liquor that they feel sure they're going to sell you to-night. These dive keepers are ready to welcome you with open arms, and they'll try to make you feel that you're royal good fellows and that they are the best friends you have in the world. Yet, to-morrow morning, how will the property be divided? The keepers of these saloons and Jim Duff will have all your money and what will you have?"

Tom paused, whipping out a white handkerchief that he deftly bound around his head, meanwhile looking miserable.

"That's what you men will have—and that's all that you'll have left," croaked the young chief engineer dismally. "Now, friends, is the game worth a candle of that sort? How many of you have money in the bank? Let every man here who has put up his hand. Not one of you? Who's keeping your money in bank for you? Jim Duff and the sellers of poisons? Will they ever hand your money back to you? Some of you men have dear ones at home. If one of these dear ones sends a hurried, frenzied appeal for money in time of sickness or death what will your answer have to be? Just this: 'I have been working like a slave for a year, but I can send you only my love. Jim Duff, who hasn't worked in all his life, won't let me send you any money.' Friends, is that what you're burning yourselves black on the desert for?"

While Tom Reade spoke Foreman Mendoza had marshaled his Mexicans and was translating the young engineer's words into Spanish.

Nor was it long ere Tom's fine presentation of the matter caught the men in the nobler part of their feelings.

"Don't blame Duff so much," Tom finally went on. "He may be a parasite, a vulture, a feeder on blood, but you and men just like you have helped to make the Duffs. You're not going to do so after this, are you, my friends? You're not going to keep the breath of life in monsters who drain you dry of life and manhood?"

"No!" came a thunderous shout, even though all of Reade's hearers did not join in it.

Even the Mexicans, listening to Mendoza's translation, became interested, despite their lesser degree of intelligence.

Tom continued to talk against time, though he wasted few words. All that he said went home to many of the laborers. While he was still talking the whistle of the pay train was heard.

Reade quickly sent his foremen and a few trusted workmen to head off any "runners" who might attempt to come in from Paloma while the men were being paid off.

As the train came to a stop Tom leaped upon a flat car behind the engine and introduced one of the newcomers—the vice president of a savings bank over in Tucson. This man, who knew the common people, talked for fifteen minutes, after which a clerk appeared from the pay car with a book in which to register the signatures of those who wished to open bank accounts. Then the paymaster and his assistants worked rapidly in paying off.

That railroad pay day proved a time of gloom to many in the town of Paloma. The returning pay train carried the bank officials and twenty-four thousand dollars that had been deposited as new accounts from the men. Of the money that remained in camp much of it was carried in the pockets of men who meant to keep it there until they received something worth while it exchange.

True, this did not trouble the majority of people in Paloma, who were sober, decent American citizens engaged in the proper walks of life.

But Jim Duff and a few others held an indignation meeting that night.

"We've been robbed!" complained one indignant saloon keeper.

"Gentlemen," observed Jim Duff, in his oiliest tones, though his face was ghastly white, "you have a new enemy, who threatens your success in business. How are you going to deal with him?"

"We'll run him off the desert, or bury him there!" came the snarling response.

"I can't believe that boy, Reade, will ever succeed in laying the railroad tracks across the Man-killer," smiled Jim Duff darkly within himself.

CHAPTER IV. SOMEBODY STIRS THE MUD

The next morning only a few of the men, some of those who had refused to open bank accounts, failed to show up at the railroad camp.

"There is really nothing to do this morning," Tom remarked to Superintendent Hawkins. "However, I think you had better dock the missing men for time off. If you find that any missing man has been gone on a proper errand of rest or enjoyment, and has not been making a beast of himself, you can restore his docked pay on the lists."

"That's a very good idea," nodded Hawkins. "It always angers me to see these poor, hardworking fellows go away and make fools of themselves just as soon as they get a bit of pay in their pockets. Still, you can't change the whole face of human nature, Mr. Reade."

"I don't expect to do so," smiled Tom. "Yet, if we can get a hundred or two in this outfit to take a sensible view of pay day, and can drill it into them so that it will stick, there will be just that number of happier men in the world. How long have you been in this work on the frontier, Mr. Hawkins?"

"About twenty years, sir."

"Then it must have angered you, many a time, to see the vultures and the parasites fattening on the men who do the real work in life."

"It has," nodded the superintendent. "However, I haven't your gift with the tongue, Mr. Reade, and I've never been able to lead men into the right path as you did yesterday."

Over in the little village of tents where the idle workmen sat through the forenoon there was some restlessness. These men knew that there was nothing for them to do until the construction material arrived, and that they were required only to report in order to keep themselves on the time sheets. Having reported to their foremen and the checkers, they were quite at liberty to go over into Paloma or elsewhere. A few of them had gone. Some others had an uneasy feeling that they wouldn't like to face the contempt in the eyes of the young chief engineer if he happened to see them going away from camp.

"It's none of the business of that chap Reade," growled one of the workmen.

"Of course it isn't," spoke up another. "He talked to us straight yesterday, however, and showed us that it was our own business to keep out of the tough places in Paloma. I've worked under these engineers for years, and I never before knew one of them to care whether I had a hundred dollars or an empty stomach. Boys, I tell you, Reade, has the right stuff in him, if he is only a youngster. He knows the enemies he has made over in Paloma, and he understands the risks be has been taking in making such enemies. He proved to us that he can stand that sort of thing and be our friend. Look at this thing, will you?"

With something of a look of wonder the speaker drew out the bankbook that he had acquired the afternoon before.

"I've got forty dollars in bank," he continued, in something of a tone of awe. "Forty friends of mine that I've put away to work and do good things for me! If I don't touch this money for some years then I'll find that this money has grown to be a lot more than forty dollars!"

22

"Or else you'll find that some bank clerk is up in Canada spending it," jeered a companion.

"I don't care what the clerk does. The bank will be still good for the money. Joe, you read the papers as often as any come into camp."

"Yes."

"All right. The next time you find anything about a savings bank that has failed and left the people in the lurch for their money, you show it to me. Savings banks don't fail nowadays! No, Sir!"

Other men through the camp were taking sly peeps at their bankbooks, as though they were half ashamed at having such possessions. Yet many a hard toiler in camp felt a new sense of importance that morning. He began to look upon himself as a part of the moneyed world as, indeed, he was!

"Telegram for Mr. Reade," called one of the two camp operators, coming forward.

Tom tore the envelope open, then stared at the following message:

"Reade, Chief Engineer.

"Have complaint from merchants of Paloma that you have effectually stopped the men from spending any money in the town. Not our policy to make enemies of the towns along our line. Explain immediately.

"(Signed) ELLSWORTH,

"General Manager."

"Hmmm!" smiled Tom, then passed the message over to Superintendent Hawkins.

"Your newly made enemies have gotten after you quickly, Sir," commented the superintendent grimly.

"Yes," nodded Tom. "And, of course, I can't follow any course that isn't approved by the general manager. I'll wire him the truth and see what he has to say. Operator!"

"Yes, Sir," replied the young man, turning and coming back.

"Wait for a message," directed Tom; then seated himself and wrote the following reply:

"Ellsworth, General Manager.

"Have not interfered in any way with honest merchants of Paloma. Men are at liberty to spend their money any way they choose. I did give the men a talk about the foolishness of spending their wages in buying liquor or in gambling. Result was that men banked about two thirds of the total pay roll with the bank people you sent on pay train yesterday at my request. Also drove off a gambler who tried to erect two tents on railroad property in order to fleece the men more speedily.

"(Signed) READE,

"Chief Engineer."

"That will tell the general manager about the kind of merchants that I've been injuring," smiled Tom, first showing the sheet to Superintendent Hawkins and then handing it to the waiting messenger.

"I hope Ellsworth, will be satisfied," nodded Hawkins. "Good will is an asset for a railway, and your enemies in Paloma may be able to stir up a good deal of trouble for you. Mr. Reade, I stood with you yesterday, and I'm still with you. If Ellsworth is so cranky that you feel like throwing the job here, then I'll walk out with you."

"Oh, I'm not going to give up the work here," predicted Reade cheerfully. "I'm too much interested in it. Neither am I going to have my hands tied by any clique of gamblers and dive keepers. If Mr. Ellsworth isn't satisfied, then I'll run up to headquarters and talk to him in person. I'm not going to quit; neither am I going to be prevented from winning and deserving the friendship of the men who are here working for us."

"Telegram for Mr. Reade," grinned the operator, again looking in at the doorway.

After reading it, Tom passed over to Hawkins this message from General Manager Ellsworth:

"Unable to judge merits of case at this distance. Will be with you soon."

"That's all right," Reade declared.

"It looks all right," muttered Hawkins, who knew something about the ways of railroads.

Up the track the whistle on a stationary engine blew the noon signal.

"Feel like eating, Harry?" Tom called to his chum, who had been mildly dozing in a chair in one corner of the room.

"Always," declared Hazelton, sitting up and yawning.

"Are you going to eat in town this noon, or in camp?" Tom inquired of the superintendent of construction.

Hawkins was about to answer that he'd eat in camp, when he suddenly reconsidered.

"I guess I'll ride along with you, Mr. Reade," he said dryly.

Horses were brought, and the three mounted and rode away. In such sizzling heat as beat down from the noonday sun Tom had not the heart to urge his mount to speed. The trio were soon at the edge of Paloma, which they had to enter through one of the streets occupied by the rougher characters.

Just as they rode down by the first buildings a low whistle sounded on the heavy, dead air.

"Signal that the locomotive is headed this way," announced Hawkins grimly. "Look out for the crossing, Mr. Reade!"

Hardly had the superintendent finished speaking when a sharp hiss sounded from an open window. Then another and more hisses, from different buildings.

"A few snakes left in the grass," Tom remarked jokingly.

"Oh, you've stirred up a nest of 'em, Mr. Reade," rejoined the superintendent.

Tom laughed as Harry added:

"Let's hope that there are no poisonous reptiles among them. It would be rough on poisonous snakes to have Tom find them."

Then the three horsemen turned the corner near the Mansion House. Superintendent Hawkins looked grave as he noted a crowd before the hotel.

"Mr. Reade, I believe those men are there waiting to see you. I'm certain they've not gathered just to talk about the weather."

24

There was a movement in the crowd, and a suppressed, surly murmur, as the engineer party was sighted.

Tom Reade, however, rode forward at the head of his party, alighting close to the crowd, which numbered fifty or sixty men. The young chief engineer signed to one of the stable boys, who came forward, half reluctantly, and took the bridles of the three horses to lead them away.

Jim Duff, backed by three other men, stepped forward. There was a world of menace in the gambler's wicked eyes as he began, in a soft, almost purring tone:

"Mr. Reade," announced Jim Duff, "we are a committee, appointed by citizens, to express our belief that the air of Paloma is not going to be good for you. At the same time we wish to ask you concerning your plans for leaving the town."

There could be no question as to the meaning of the speaker. Tom Reade was being ordered out of town.

CHAPTER V. TOM HAS NO PLANS FOR LEAVING TOWN

"My plans for leaving town?" repeated Tom pleasantly. "Why, gentlemen, I'll meet your question frankly by saying that I haven't made any such plans."

"You're going to do so, aren't?" inquired Duff casually.

"By the time that my partner and I have finished our work for the road, Mr. Duff, I imagine that we shall be making definite plans to go away, unless the railroad officials decide to keep us here with Paloma as headquarters for other work."

"We believe that it would be much better for your health if you went away at once," Duff insisted, with a mildness that did not disguise his meaning in the least.

Tom deemed it not worth while to pretend any longer that he did not understand.

"Oh, then it's a case of 'Here's your hat. What's your hurry?'" asked Reade smilingly.

"Something in that line," assented Jim Duff. "I venture to assure you that we are quite in earnest in our anxiety for your welfare, Mr. Reade."

"Whom do you men represent?" asked Tom.

"The citizens of Paloma," returned Duff.

"All of them?" Reade insisted.

"All of them—with few exceptions."

"I understand you, of course," Tom nodded.

"Now, Mr. Duff, I'll tell you what I propose. I'm curious to know just how many there are on your side of the fence. Pardon me, but I really can't quite believe that the better citizens of this town are behind you. I know too many Arizona men, and I have too good an opinion of them. Your kind of crowd makes a lot of noise at times, and the other kind of Arizona crowd rarely makes any noise. I know, of course, the element in the town that your committee represents, but I don't believe that your element is by any means in the majority here."

"I assure you that we represent the sentiment of the town," Duff retorted steadily.

"Much as I regret the necessity for seeming to slight your opinion," Tom went on with as pleasant a smile as at first, "I call for a showing of hands or a count of noses. I'll tell you what we'll do, Mr. Duff, if it meets with your approval. We'll hire a hall, sharing the expense. We'll state the question fairly in the local newspaper, and we'll invite all good citizens to turn out, meet in the hall, hear the case on both sides, and then decide for themselves whether they want the railroad engineers to leave the town or—"

"They do want you to leave town!" the gambler insisted.

"Or whether they want Jim Duff and some of his friends to leave town," Tom Reade continued good-humoredly.

Jim Duff turned, gazing back at the men with him. They represented the roughest element in the town.

"No use arguing with a mule, Jim!" growled a red-faced man at the rear of the crowd. "Get a rail, boys, and we'll start the procession right now."

"Bring a rope along, too!" called another man hoarsely.

"Get two rails and one rope!" proposed a third bad character. "The other kid doesn't seem to be sassy enough to need a rope."

"Gentlemen," broke in Harry Hazelton gravely, "if anyone of you imagines that I'm holding my tongue because I disapprove of my partner's course, let me assure you that I back every word he says."

"Make it two ropes, then!" jeered another voice.

"Reade," continued Jim Duff, "we all try to be decent men here, and the friends with me are a good and sensible lot of men. You have carried matters just a little too far. Think over what you've heard and noticed here, and then tell me again about your plans, for quitting Paloma."

As he spoke Jim made a gesture that kept some of the men near him from rushing forward. Tom did not appear to notice the demonstration at all. Certainly he did not flinch.

"I haven't any such plans," Tom laughed. "I'm hungry and I'm going inside to eat."

With that, he turned his back on the crowd, with Harry behind him, both making for the steps of the hotel. Superintendent Hawkins stepped in after the boys.

"Gentlemen, I can't do anything more," spoke up Jim Duff, with an air of resignation.

"But we can!" roared some of the roughs in the crowd. A dozen of them surged forward. The first of them swung a lariat to slip it over Tom Reade's neck.

Bump! Hawkins's sledge-hammer right hand shot out, landing on that fellow's face. With a moan the fellow collapsed on the sidewalk, his jaw broken.

Then Tom and Harry wheeled like a flash, eyeing the idlers and roughs sternly.

"Don't go any further," proposed Tom, his eyes growing steely, "unless you mean it."

26

Something in the attitude of the trio of athletic figures standing ready before them disquieted the crowd of roughs. There were armed men in that crowd, but all felt that they had been put in the wrong, so far, and none of them dared draw the first weapon or fire the first shot.

"Take that injured man to a surgeon and have his jaw set," spoke Tom quietly. "Let the surgeon send me the bill. I'm sorry for the fellow, for I'm indirectly the cause of his being hurt. The main cause of his misfortune was due to his being in bad company."

"Come out of that hotel," ordered Jim Duff, his eyes blazing as he stepped forward, though with Hawkins's cold, hard eyes on him the gambler was careful to keep his hands at his sides. "You can't get anything to eat in there!"

"Do you own the hotel?" Tom inquired coolly.

"No; but you can't eat there."

"Join us at lunch, Mr. Hawkins!" Tom invited, turning away from the gambler. The superintendent nodded, for he had no intention of leaving the young engineers for the present.

All three entered the hotel, while the small mob outside hooted and jeered. Tom led the way to a table in the dining room, signing to one of the waiters.

Hardly had the waiter reached them when Jim Duff and the proprietor of the Mansion House came in. Jim, after saying a few words in a low tone, halted, while the proprietor came forward.

"Good morning, Mr. Ashby," nodded Tom, when he saw the proprietor headed their way. The latter looked rather embarrassed, but he moved a hand to signal the waiter to withdraw.

"I'm sorry, Mr. Reade, but I can't have you any longer at this hotel," began Ashby.

"Any particular reason?" Tom inquired, looking the man straight in the eye.

"Yes; some of my other guests object to your presence here."

"Meaning Jim Duff?" questioned Reade coolly.

"I don't care to discuss the matter with you, Mr. Reade, but I can't entertain you here any longer."

"Does that apply even to this meal, Mr. Ashby?"

"It does."

"Very good," nodded Tom, rising. Harry and Hawkins shoved their chairs back, too, and stood up.

"Say, but I don't like the looks of that!" announced a voice from another table. There were five men seated there, all of them well-dressed and prosperous-looking traveling salesmen, who had arrived that morning.

"This is a very regrettable necessity on my part, gentlemen," began Proprietor Ashby hurriedly, and plainly ill at ease. "Some of my regular guests object to the presence of these young men, and so—"

"These young gentlemen have gotten in bad by objecting to having their men fleeced here in town, haven't they?" inquired the boldest of the drummers. "I heard something about it this morning."

"Perhaps you haven't heard all the circumstances," suggested Ashby in growing embarrassment.

"We've heard enough, anyway," replied the same drummer briskly. "So these young men, who are a credit to their profession and to their home towns, are ordered to leave here? Boys, I guess we leave, too, don't we?"

The other traveling salesmen assented emphatically.

Now Proprietor Ashby felt dismal, indeed. These five men were occupying the best quarters in his hotel, outside of those occupied by Jim Duff. It was not the loss of patronage from these men alone that troubled Ashby. Traveling salesmen have their own ways of "passing around the word" and downing any hotel that depends largely on their patronage.

"You can have all our rooms, then, Mr. Ashby," proposed the same drummer. "We'll have our things out and be ready for our bills within twenty minutes."

"But, gentlemen, be calm about this," begged Ashby. "Finish your meals first. There may be some way of arranging—"

"There is," returned the drummer, with a smile that was a fine duplicate of Tom's own. "We know just where to arrange for the kind of accommodations that we want. Mr. Reade," turning to Tom and Harry, "will you allow me to introduce ourselves. We are aching to shake hands with you, for we've heard all about you."

Proprietor Ashby fidgeted at the side, while the eight departing guests paused long enough to make their names known to each other.

Jim Duff had vanished early, leaving the hotel man to his own humiliation.

The introductions concluded, Hawkins followed the young engineers to their room while the drummers went to their own more costly quarters and hastily packed their belongings.

Fifteen minutes later the party stood in the office and porters were bringing down trunks. Tom and Harry, keeping most of their belongings at camp, had only suit cases to carry.

"Gentlemen, I think you are making a mistake," began Mr. Ashby, as he met the salesmen in the lobby near the clerk's desk.

"We made a mistake in coming here," retorted the leader of the salesmen, pleasantly as to tone, "but we're rectifying it now. Are our bills ready?"

The proprietor went behind the desk to make change, while the clerk receipted seven bills. Ashby's hands shook as he manipulated the money.

"Dobson," he said, in a low tone to one of the drummers, "I had intended ordering a ton of hams from you. Now, of course, I can't—"

"Quite right," nodded Mr. Dobson cheerfully. "You couldn't get them from our house at four times the market price. We wouldn't want our brand served here."

The last bill was paid. Proprietor Ashby stiffened, his backbone, trying to look game.

"Gentlemen," he inquired, "where are you going from here? Won't you let me call the 'bus to take you?"

"Never mind the 'bus, Ash," smilingly replied the leader of the drummers, a man named Pritchard. "If you'll send the 'bus over to the Cactus House with our trunks we'll be greatly obliged."

"Certainly, gentlemen, it's a pleasure to oblige you," murmured Ashby, with a ghastly effort to look pleasant. He watched the eight men step outside. Duff and his crowd had vanished. It would never do to try any mob tricks on so many strangers who had done nothing. The most easy-going citizens of an Arizona town would turn out to punish such a mob.

The three railroad men had their horses brought around, but they rode slowly, chatting with the salesmen on the sidewalk.

In this order they reached the Cactus House, which, thirty years ago, had been famous in and around the old Paloma of the frontier days. The proprietor, a young man named Carter, had succeeded his father in the ownership of the property. It was a neat hotel, but a small one. The elder Carter had lost a good deal of money before his death, and the son was now trying to build up the property with hardly any reserve capital.

At the Cactus there was a great flurry when five such important guests arrived and the young railroad engineers were also most heartily welcomed.

"Our meal time is nearly over, but I'll have something special cooked for you right away, gentlemen," cried young Carter, bustling about, his eyes aglow.

"Before you get that meal ready," said Pritchard, drawing young Carter aside, "I want to ask you whether any man can ever be driven from this hotel, just for being decent?"

"He certainly cannot," replied Proprietor Carter with emphasis.

"Live up to that, son," advised the drummer, "and I half suspect that you'll prosper."

The meal finished, the three men from the railroad camp took leave of their new salesmen friends, mounted and rode back to camp.

"The snakes are not all dead yet," mused Tom quizzically, as, in riding through the "tough" street again they heard hisses from open windows at which no heads appeared.

"There's a letter here for you, Mr. Reade," announced Foreman Payson, who was sitting alone in the office.

"Who brought it?"

"I don't know his name. Never saw him before. He rode out here on horseback."

The envelope, though a good one as to quality, was dirty on the outside. Tom Reade hastily broke the seal and read:

"If you don't get away from Paloma pretty soon your presence will hold the railroad up for a longtime to come! Get out, if you're wise, or the railroad will suffer with you!"

"I reckon the fellow who wrote that was sincere enough," said Tom, as he passed the letter over to his chum. "However, I don't like to feel that I can be seared by any man who's too cowardly to sign his name to a letter."

CHAPTER VI. THE GENERAL MANAGER "LOOKS IN"

Neither Tom nor Harry was stupid enough to be wholly unafraid over the threats of the day. Both realized that Jim Duff and the latter's associates were ugly and treacherous men who would fight sooner than be deprived of their chance to fleece the railway workmen. Yet neither young engineer had any intention of being scared into flight.

"They'll put up a lot of trouble for us," said Tom that afternoon, as the two chums talked the matter over. "They may even go to extremities, and—"

"Shoot us?" smiled Hazelton, though there was a serious look under his smile.

"Yes; they may even try that," I nodded Tom. "Though they won't make an open attempt. They may try to get us from ambush at night. They will be desperate, though not over brave. Recollect, Harry, that the better element in Paloma won't stand much nonsense. There are no braver men in the world than are found right in Arizona, and no men more decent."

"Barring Duff and his gang," laughed Hazelton.

"They're not real Arizona men. They're the kind of human vultures who flock after large pay rolls in any place where men work without having their families in near-by homes. If Duff had enough men of his own way of thinking, they might try to ride out here to camp and clean us out. If they did, then all the decent men in this part of Arizona would take to the saddle and drive Duff and his crew into hiding. After what happened to-day you won't find Duff daring to do anything too open."

"Excuse me, Sir, but there's a train coming," reported Foreman Rivers, thrusting his head in at the doorway of the little office building.

"Not a construction train?" Reade asked.

"Can't make it out yet, sir. The whistle was reported a minute ago."

Tom and Harry, chafing a good deal under their enforced idleness while waiting for materials, hastened outdoors. Soon the train was close enough to be made out. It consisted of an engine, baggage car and one private car.

"It's one or more of the road's officials," murmured Harry.

"I hope it's Mr. Ellsworth," replied Reade, as the chums walked briskly down to the spot where the train would have to halt.

It turned out to be the general manager, a big and capable-looking man of fifty, with a belt-line just a trifle too large for comfort, who swung himself to the ground the instant that the train stopped.

"I'm glad you're here, Reade," nodded the general manager, as he caught sight of his two young engineers. "Come back into my car. We can talk better there."

Tom and Harry mounted to the platform of the car, following Mr. Ellsworth down the carpeted aisle of a very comfortable private Pullman car. The general manager pointed to seats, threw himself into another, and then said:

"Now, tell me all about the row that you've started with the town."

Harry's lips closed tightly, but Tom launched at once into a plain, truthful account of the affair, bringing it down to the noonday meal of the present day.

"It's not clear to me just why you should feel called upon to interfere so forcefully," said the general manager, a little fretfully. "The workmen are all twenty-one years of age and upwards. Couldn't they protect themselves if they wanted protection?"

"Yes, sir, certainly," Tom admitted. "However, letting that fellow Duff put up his tents right on the railroad property would almost make it look as though the road shared, or at least approved, his enterprise."

"Oh, doubtless you were right to order the fellow off the railroad property," assented Mr. Ellsworth. "But why did you go to such trouble to get the men to start new bank accounts and thus send most of their money out of town?"

"May I answer that question, sir, by asking another?" asked Reade respectfully. "Did you wish the men to spend it in Paloma?"

"I don't care a hang what they do with it," retorted the general manager half peevishly. "It's their own money."

"It was you, Mr. Ellsworth, whom I wired yesterday morning, asking that you send down a representative of a savings bank who could open accounts with such of the men as desired."

"Yes, and I sent you a couple of bank men. I didn't have any idea, however, that you'd get the whole town of Paloma by the ears."

"I haven't, sir. I assure you of that. I've hurt only a few parasites—a flock of human vultures. The decent people of the town don't side with them."

"I wish I could be sure that we haven't offended the town as a whole," mused Mr. Ellsworth, "The good will of the people along our line is a great asset."

"You're acquainted with a lot of the real people in Paloma, aren't you, Mr. Ellsworth?"

"With some of them, yes."

"Then, while you're here, sir, I'd be glad if you'd look up some of these acquaintances in town and find out for yourself just how the sentiment stands. We don't wish you to feel that we're a pair of trouble-makers who are doing our best to ruin the road with its future customers."

"I believe I will go into town," mused Mr. Ellsworth. "Is there an automobile anywhere about here?"

"No, sir; but our telegraph operator can wire into town for one. It will take but a few minutes to have a car here."

"Send for it, then."

"Would you like to see Mr. Hawkins while you're waiting, sir?" Tom suggested, rising. "You know Hawkins, and probably you'll be satisfied with his judgment."

"Send Hawkins along."

"Yes, sir; and we won't return for the present, unless you send for us," Reade replied, going toward the forward end of the car.

Superintendent Hawkins was closeted with the general manager until the arrival of the automobile. There was a frown on Mr. Ellsworth's face as they started townward.

"Well," asked Harry Hazelton, with a grin on his face, as he watched the departing car, "are we going to be fired or praised?"

"We're going to lay the track across the Man-killer," returned Reade resolutely.

"How about the gambler and his bad crowd? Are we going to beat them?"

"We're going to do whatever the general manager orders, just as long as we remain here," replied Tom. "He's our only source of authority. If he tells me to let Jim Duff bring a cityful of tents out here and run night or day—then that's all there will be to it."

"I'd sooner quit," growled Hazelton, "than knuckle to such a crew of rascals."

"So would I," nodded Tom good-humoredly, "if it were my quit. But, if Mr. Ellsworth gives such orders it will be his quit, not ours."

Harry walked restlessly up and down the little office, but Tom threw himself down at full length on a cot in the corner. Within two minutes he was sound asleep.

"Humph!" growled Hazelton, as soon as he saw his chum's unconcern. Then he went outside to finish his tramp.

It was toward the close of the afternoon when Mr. Ellsworth returned. Harry was out of sight as the general manager stepped directly into the office.

"Reade," he began. Deep breathing from the corner greeted him. General Manager Ellsworth gazed down at the sleeping form, and a new light of admiration dawned in his eyes.

"So that's the young man whom they're talking of shooting, poisoning or blowing into the next world with dynamite?" he thought. "A lot this young man appears to think about his enemies! There's real courage in this young man. Reade, wake up—if you can spare the time."

Tom opened his eyes, rubbed them, then sat up, next springing to his feet.

"Not having any real work to do makes me sleepy," laughed Tom good-naturedly. "I trust you didn't have to call me many times, Mr. Ellsworth?"

The general manager held out his hand.

"Reade, I've just learned in town what a plucky thing you did, and how coolly you went through it all. A young man with your courage and purpose simply can't be fool enough to be very far wrong."

"Then you learned that the real Arizona people over in Paloma don't find any fault with what I did?" queried Tom.

"Reade, what I discovered is that you have a lot of the finest manhood in Arizona just wild with respect for you," declared Mr. Ellsworth. Then the general manager lowered his voice before he resumed:

"At the same time, Reade, I've also learned that you've stirred up such an evil nest of rattlers that you'll be fortunate if you escape with your life. Candidly, if you feel that you'd like to leave here—"

"Do you want me to quit, sir?" demanded Tom, looking steadily into his chief's eyes.

"I don't," declared Mr. Ellsworth promptly. "If you and Hazelton were to quit me now I don't know where I could get another pair of men who could put into the work all the skill and energy that you two employ."

"Did you have dinner in town, sir?" Tom asked.

"No, for I came out to take you two young men in. Hawkins will also be with us at dinner this evening. He has told me about the Mansion House affair, so the Cactus House shall be the railway house hereafter. That fellow Ashby is uneasy; I think he will be more than uneasy after a while."

The dinner party motored back to town. Dinner was more like a reception that evening, for the news of Tom's plucky fight against the rough element had spread through the town. Nearly two score of men representing the better part of the population of Paloma called at the hotel to shake hands with the young engineers.

"They don't seem to care a hang about me, these men, do they, Hawkins?" laughed the general manager, as he and the superintendent stood in the background of the picture.

"That's because they're Arizona men, sir," replied Hawkins. "Their interest is in the man who has done the thing, not in the boss."

"I can understand why President Newnham, of the S. B. & L., recommended these young men so extravagantly. They're full of force and absolutely free from self-conceit."

Finally the party motored back towards the camp. As it was after dark now, some of the citizens who had visited them escorted the slow moving car as far as the edge of the town, but none of Jim Duff's followers appeared on the streets through which they passed.

"Why are we going back to camp, anyway?" demanded Mr. Ellsworth. "Why not sleep at the hotel to-night?"

"Why, I think it may be better for you to go back to the hotel, sir," Tom proposed. "As for Harry and myself, after what has happened in town to-day, it may be as well if we are on hand at the camp to-night. There may be some attempt to stampede our men. The crowd in Paloma are capable of offering our men free drink, just to do us mischief. We've a lot of strong men in our force, but there are some weak vessels who would be caught by a free offer, and some of our work gangs would be demoralized to-morrow."

Mr. Ellsworth thereupon decided to return to the camp also, and, arriving there, dismissed the car. A tent was pitched for him close to the office, and a cot rigged up in it.

Then the party sat up, chatting, after most of the workmen had turned in for the night.

"I'll be thankful when the material gets here," sighed Tom. "I'm tired of loafing."

"It seems to me that you have been doing anything but loafing," smiled the general manager.

"I want to get to work on the Man-killer. Besides, idleness is costing the road a lot of money in wages for these men."

"I wired this afternoon," stated Mr. Ellsworth, "to have the material trains rushed forward on express schedule as soon as the stuff strikes our lines."

"Then—" began Hawkins slowly.

His next words were drowned out by a booming explosion to the westward of the camp.

"The scoundrels!" gasped Tom Reade, leaping up. "This is more of our friends' work! They have dynamited the most ticklish part of the work on the Man-killer!"

CHAPTER VII. A DYNAMITE PUZZLE

"The scoundrels!" cried General Manager Ellsworth.

He was a man who believed in working along easy lines when possible. His career as a railroad man had taught him the value of meeting other people half way. Now the general manager's white face and flashing eyes revealed the fighter in him.

From off to the south, beyond the quicksand, came a chorus of sharp, shrill, gleeful whoops.

"There go the curs!" flared Harry.

Another volley of jeers reached the camp officials.

"They are mounted on horses," spoke Tom judicially. "They couldn't travel as fast on foot and yell at the same time."

A third taunting chorus traveled over the desert. But Tom and his friends, in the darkness of the night, could not make out the horsemen nor judge how many there were of them.

"You'd better turn out the camp, Mr. Hawkins," directed Tom in a calmer voice.

The superintendent ran over to where a night engineer almost dozed at his post beside a stationary engine.

Half a minute later a series of shrill blasts rang out over the camp. Laborers came tumbling out of the tents. Many of them had slept so soundly that even the noise of dynamiting they had regarded only as a part of their dreams. But the whistle meant business.

"Get the torches out, Mr. Rivers," called Tom, as one of the foremen reported on a run.

To Foreman Payson, Harry gave the order to marshal a hundred of the men to remain in and around the camp, alertly watchful.

"That's a good idea," nodded Mr. Ellsworth. "The explosion may be only a trick to, empty the camp, as a prelude to further mischief."

Scores of torches flared in the darkness as the workmen hurried westward. At the head of all went Tom Reade and the general manager.

Less than half a mile away they came upon the scene of mischief.

"It's just what I expected," nodded Tom, as the leading party halted under the flare of the torches. "You see, sir, here was the point of greatest cave and drift in the quicksand. It's where your former engineers found such a morass of the shifty stuff that they declared the Man-killer never could have its appetite satisfied with dirt. There was a good log and concrete foundation laid down there, and for thirty-six hours the sand had not shifted a particle as far as the eye could discover. Now, look at it!"

Before them the top layer of desert sand had sunk away, revealing a well or sink, one hundred and fifty feet across and the bottom at least forty feet below the general level.

"I always wondered why a suspension bridge wouldn't solve the problem more easily and cheaply than any other construction," muttered Mr. Ellsworth, after he had gotten over his first indignation.

"To avoid every possibility of lurking quicksand the suspension bridge would have to be more than a mile long," Reade answered. "Beyond, there are other treacherous little patches of quicksand. It would cost the road millions to put up a suspension bridge that would hold.

"A short bridge would look all right and doubtless serve all right, for a while. Then, some fine day, part of the structure would give, and a trainload of passengers would be sucked down and out of sight by the shifting sands of the Man-killer."

Mr. Ellsworth turned aside with a shudder.

"I'm glad I'm not an engineer," he said earnestly. "The responsibility for safety of life at this point is all yours, Reade."

"And I'm willing enough to take it, sir, if you don't run trains over the Man-killer until the new roadbed has stood tests that I'll put upon it."

"It'll cost at least ten thousand dollars to repair the mischief that the scoundrels have done to-night," figured Harry Hazelton thoughtfully.

"Then, if we can find out the guilty wretches for certain, we'll see that they earn more than that amount by enforced labor in prison,'" retorted the general manager grimly.

"Mr. Bell!" called Tom briskly.

"Here, sir," reported the foreman, coming forward..

"Mr. Bell, I wish you'd pick out twenty-one good men. Make the brightest of the lot head of the new force of night watchmen. Place the other twenty under his orders. Your gangs will come into play here later than the others, so I'll let your shift of men have the first chance at night-watchman duty."

"All right, sir," nodded Foreman Bell. "Any further orders?"

"None, except that your watchmen will do their best to guard both the line of roadbed and the camp. Further, tell the night engineer to be sure to have steam up so that he can blow a lot of signals at anytime in the night."

"Very good, sir," and the foreman hurried away.

"I'm disgusted with myself for having been caught in this fashion," Tom admitted to Mr. Ellsworth. "But I hadn't an idea that Paloma held any dynamite. I can't imagine how a frontier town on the alkali desert needs dynamite."

"It will probably be found that someone shipped it in a hurry," suggested Mr. Ellsworth.

"But how? Any fellow would be detected who had it brought in on our trains. There has been no time to I stage I it from any other point since the row with Duff started."

"It's a puzzle," admitted Mr. Ellsworth.

"It is, but it won't be for long," Reade declared confidently. "There are ways of finding out how that dynamite got into Paloma, there must be ways of finding out who caused it to be brought in."

Then, suddenly, Tom's eyes grew wider open and brighter.

"Mr. Ellsworth, I believe that dynamite was brought in before the trouble opened."

"But who would have wished to bring dynamite here until the trouble started?"

"Anyone might be interested in doing it who wanted to see trouble start."

"I'm afraid I don't follow you, Reade," observed the general manager, frowning slightly.

"There were others who wanted the job of blocking the Man-killer," Tom went on earnestly. "They wanted a lot more money for the job than we thought was necessary. I don't want to accuse anyone, but I am just a trifle suspicious that the concern of Chicago contractors—"

"The Colthwaite people!" broke in Mr. Ellsworth.

"Yes; if they were bad people, and ugly business rivals—"

"How would the Colthwaite people be able to foresee that you were going to have a fight with Jim Duff?" interposed Mr. Ellsworth.

"I'm going after the answer, if there is one. I hope to be able to tell you the answer one of these days."

Tom and Harry made two trips each, in different directions, to make sure that the watch men were awake and alert. It was nearly eleven o'clock when the general manager and his engineers turned in for a night's rest—"subject to the approval of Jim Duff," as Tom dryly stated it.

No more interruptions followed during the night, however. At daylight the watchmen sought their tents and the day force began to stir soon after.

After the steam whistle bad blown the breakfast call, Reade slipped away from his friends to inspect the laborers at the meal.

"There are some of your men absent, Mr. Mendoza," Tom murmured to the Mexican foreman.

"Yes, Senor. Some of my men slipped away in the night."

"Went off to Paloma, eh?"

Mendoza shrugged his shoulders.

"Gambling, drinking—both," nodded Tom.

"Undoubtedly, Senor."

"Get the names of your absent Mexicans, and report to me with them."

Reade then went to the other foremen, with the same orders.

Before Tom had seated himself at his own meal, with Harry and Mr. Ellsworth, the foremen appeared, lists in their hands. Tom rapidly ran his finger down the lists.

"Twenty-eight Mexicans and fourteen Americans absent from camp," he muttered. "Foremen, when these men come back you may tell them that they are no longer needed."

All four of the gang bosses looked somewhat astonished.

"Merely for leaving camp in the night time?" Mendoza inquired.

"Yes, under the circumstances," nodded Tom. "If any of these men declare that they were properly absent, and did not visit the gambling and the drinking dives, then such men may be reinstated after they have satisfied Mr. Hazelton, Mr. Hawkins or myself of the truth of their statements."

"Some of these men will be very ugly when they find that they are discharged, Senor," suggested Mendoza.

"But you are loyal to us?"

"Can you doubt it, Senor?" asked Mendoza proudly.

"Then you will know how to handle your own fellow-countrymen. The other foremen will be able to handle the rest of the disgruntled ones. However, as I have told you, if any man claims that he is unjustly treated, send him to headquarters for a chance at reinstatement."

General Manager Ellsworth had heard the conversation, but had not interfered. As soon as the young engineers were alone he joined them at table, saying:

"Aren't you afraid, Reade, that these discharged men will hasten to join our enemies?"

"That is very likely, sir," Tom answered. "These missing men, however, have shown their willingness to become our enemies by leaving camp and seeking their pleasures in the strongholds of the scoundrels who are fighting to break us up."

"That's another way of looking at the matter," assented the general manager.

"I'd much rather have our enemies outside of camp than inside," Reade continued. "If we took these absentees back after they've been in the company of rascals, then we wouldn't have any means of knowing how many of the absentees had agreed to do treacherous things within the camp. It would hardly be a wise plan to encourage the breeding of rattlesnakes within the camp limits."

It was nearly noon when the first batch of laborers, some American and some Mexican, returned to camp. These men started to go by the checker's hut at a distance, but keen-eyed Superintendent Hawkins saw them and ordered them around to the hut.

"You'll have to wait here until your foremen are called," declared the checker.

"Say, what's the trouble here!" demanded one American belligerently.

CHAPTER VIII. READE MEETS A "KICKER" HALF WAY

"Who's your foreman?" asked the checker, a young fellow named Royal

"Payson—if it's any of your business." replied the workman roughly.

The others, seeing him take this attitude, were willing to let him talk for all. Superintendent Hawkins had rounded up the foremen, and now sent them to the checker's hut to deal with the men.

"Some of you are my men," said Payson, looking the lot over. "You're discharged."

"What's that?" roared the same indignant spokesman, a big, bull-necked, red-faced fellow.

"Discharged," said Payson briefly. "All of you who belong to my gang. Checker, I'll call their names off to you."

While Payson, and then the other foremen, were calling the names, the workmen stood by in sullen silence. When the last name had been entered the same bull-necked spokesman flared up again.

"Have we no rights?" he demanded. "Is there no such thing as the right of appeal in this camp, or are we under a lot of domineering, petty tyrants like you?"

"I'm a poor specimen of tyrant,'" laughed Payson good-naturedly. "All I'm doing, Bellas, is following orders. Any man who feels that he was justified in being away, and that he ought to be kept on the pay rolls here, may make his appeal to Mr. Hawkins, Mr. Hazelton or Mr. Reade."

"I'll see Reade!" announced Bellas stiffly. "That youngster is doing all the dirty work here. I'll go to him straight."

"I'll take you over to his office," nodded Foreman Payson.

"I'm going, too," announced another workman.

"So'm I," added another.

"One at a time, men," advised Payson. "I think Bellas feels that he's capable of talking for all of you."

The other foremen restrained the crowd, while Mr. Payson led Bellas over to the headquarters shack.

Tom looked up from a handful of old letters as the two men entered.

"See here, you!" was Bellas's form of greeting.

"Try it again," smiled Tom pleasantly.

"You're the man I want to talk to," Bellas snarled. "What do you mean by—"

"What's your name?" asked Reade quickly.

"None of your—"

"We can never do business on that kind of courtesy," smiled Reade. "Mr. Payson, show the man out and let him come back when he's cooler."

"There isn't anyone here who can show me out!" blustered Bellas, swinging his big arms and causing the heavy muscles to stand out.

"If you don't care to behave in a businesslike way, and talk like a man, we'll do our best to show you out," Tom retorted, still with a pleasant smile. "What are you here for, anyway?"

"Why have I been fired?" roared Bellas.

"Can't you guess?" queried Tom.

"Was it for going to town and being away all night?"

"Yes, and also for not being on hand this morning."

"There wasn't any work to do," growled Bellas.

"You expected to be paid for your time, and you should have been in camp, as your time belonged to the railroad by, right of purchase. Bellas, you have been drinking over in town, haven't you?"

"If I have, it's my own business. I'm no slave."

"Ben gambling, too?"

"None of your—"

"You're in error," Tom answered pleasantly, though firmly. "The gamblers over in Paloma are leagued with the dive keepers against us, Bellas. You know what they did out at the big sink of the Man-killer last night. Any man who goes away from camp and 'enjoys' himself for hours among those who are trying to put us out of business shows himself to be a friend to the enemies of this camp. Therefore the man who does that shows himself to be one of our enemies, in sympathy if not in fact."

"I'm no lawyer," growled Bellas sullenly, "and I can't follow your flow of gab."

"You know well enough what I'm saying to you, Bellas, and you know that I'm right. Since you've been away and joined our enemies we don't want you here.

38

More, we don't intend to have you here. Mr. Payson has dropped you from the rolls, and that cuts you off from this camp. Now, I think you will understand that it is some of our business whether you have been over in town emptying your pockets, into Jim Duff's hat. If that is what you have been doing, then we don't want you here, and won't have you. If you haven't been hob-nobbing with our enemies, and paying all you had for the privilege, then we'll look into any claims of better conduct that you may make, and, if satisfied that you've been telling the truth, we'll reinstate you."

"Oh, you make me tired—you kid!" burst from Bellas's lips.

"This isn't an experience meeting," Tom replied, not losing his smile, "and I'm not interested in your impressions of me. Do you wish to make any statement advocating your right to be taken on the pay roll again?"

"No, I don't!" roared the angry fellow. "All I want to do is to show you my opinion of you, Tommy! I can do that best by rubbing your nose in the dirt outside."

Foreman Payson flung himself between the big, angry human bull and the young chief engineer.

"Don't waste any time or heat on him, Mr. Payson," Tom advised, slipping his handful of letters into his coat and tossing that garment to the back of the room. "If Bellas has any grudge against me, I don't want to stop him from making his last kick."

Tom took a step forward, his open hands hanging at his sides. He didn't look by any means alarmed, though Bellas appeared to be about twice the young chief engineer's size.

So prompt had been Reade's action that, for a moment, Bellas looked astounded. Then, with a roar, he leaped forward, swinging both arms and closing in.

Tom Reade had had his best physical training on the football gridiron. He dropped, instantly, as he leaped forward, making a low tackle and rising with both arms wrapped around Bellas's knees. Tom took two swift steps forward, then heaved his man, head first, out through the open doorway.

Bellas landed about eight feet away. He was not hurt, beyond a jolting, and leaped to his feet, shaking both fists.

"Not unless you really insist upon it," smiled Tom, shaking his head. "It's too warm for exercise to-day."

"You tricky little whipper-snapper!" roared Bellas, making an angry bound for the doorway.

Tom met his angry rush. Both went down, rolling over and over on the ground. Bellas wound his powerful arms about the boy, and would have crushed him. Though Tom hated to do it, there was no alternative but to choke the powerful bully. Bellas soon let go, dazed and gasping. Ere the big fellow came to his senses sufficiently to know what he was about, Reade had hoisted Bellas to one shoulder.

Down by the checker's hut the crowd of curious workmen gasped as they saw Tom Reade jogging along with this great load over one shoulder. Reaching the line, Tom gave another heave. Bellas rolled on the ground. He was conscious and could have gotten up, but he chose to lay where he had fallen and think matters over.

"Don't think I'm peevish, men," Tom called pleasantly. "I wouldn't have done that if Bellas hadn't attacked me. I had to defend myself. Now, while I'm here, does any man wish to make a claim for justice? Does any man feel that he has been discharged unfairly?"

Three or four men answered, though none of the Mexicans was among the number. When questioned as to whether they had spent the night among Jim Duff's friends all the speakers admitted that they had. Tom then made them the same explanation he had offered Bellas.

"That's about all that can be said, isn't it, men?" Tom asked in conclusion. "I am sorry for those of you who feel hurt, but while there is bad blood in the air every man must choose between one camp or the other. You men chose Jim Duff, and you'll have to abide by your choice."

"But we haven't any money," declared one of the men sullenly.

"Now you're just beginning to understand that Jim Duff won't be a very good friend to a penniless man. Didn't you know that when you shook all your change into his hat?"

"Are you going to let us starve?" growled the man.

"You won't starve, nor need you be out of work long," Tom retorted. "Any man who can do the work of a railway laborer in this country doesn't have to remain out of a job. Now, I'll ask you to get off the railroad's ground."

Tom turned and went back to the office, while Payson and the other foremen saw to it that the discharged men left the railroad's property. In less than half an hour the disgruntled ones were back in the worst haunts of Paloma, spreading the news of Tom Reade's latest outrage.

When Tom reached the office he found Mr. Ellsworth inside.

"I saw what you did, Reade, though you didn't know I was about. You handled it splendidly. You made it plain enough, too, to the men that they had joined the enemy and thereby declared against us."

"Message, Mr. Reade," called the operator from the doorway.

"The construction material train, the first one, will be here within two hours," cried Tom, looking up from the paper, his eyes dancing. "Now we can do some of the real work that we've been waiting to do!"

CHAPTER IX. THE MAN-KILLER CLAIMS A SACRIFICE

In the days that followed Tom Reade and Harry Hazelton were more continuously and seriously busy than they had ever been before in their lives.

Sometimes it happens that engineers come upon a quicksand that apparently has no bottom. It will be filled and apparently the earth on top is solid. After a few days there will follow either a gradual shifting away or a sudden cave in, and the quicksand must once more be attacked.

This condition had been experienced more than a dozen times with the Man-killer before Tom and Harry had been called to solve the problem.

There is no definite way of attacking a quicksand. Much must depend upon the local conditions. Where it is a small one, yet of seemingly considerable depth, it is sometimes quickest and cheapest to cross it with a suspension bridge, the terminal pillars resting on sure foundations. Some quicksands are overcome by merely filling in new sand or loam, patiently, until at last the trap is blocked and a permanently solid foundation is laid. There are many other ways of overcoming the difficulty.

The method hit upon by Tom and Harry, after looking over the situation, was one that was largely original with them.

It consisted of laying logs, of different lengths, from twelve to eighteen feet, in a transverse net work filling in earth on this and allowing the structure gradually to sink where the quicksand shifted or caved. The sideway drift, at some points, was overcome by hollow steel piles, driven in as firmly as might be, and then filled with cement from the top. A line of such piles when imbedded in the ground, helps to make an effective block to side drift.

At the outset a few feet of these steel piles were left exposed above the surface, their gradual settling serving as a reliable index to the evasive movements of the extensive quicksand underneath. At other points wooden piles were driven in for the same purpose.

General Manager Ellsworth did not spend all his time in camp. He could not do so, in fact, for he had many other pressing duties. However, he ran over frequently, and always appeared satisfied.

"Of course it's too early to talk confidently, Reade," said Mr. Ellsworth, one day when the work had been going on steadily for some weeks, "but I believe you have the only right method. I have so reported to our directors. You'll have disappointments, of course, but I hope you'll encounter none that you can't overcome."

"I shan't crow until I've seen the test applied to the roadbed over the Man-killer," Tom replied thoughtfully. "After I've seen that test applied a couple of times then I'm ready to go before any board and swear that the Man-killer has been tamed for all time."

"Speed the day!" replied Mr. Ellsworth, as he climbed into his private car to return. "By the way, you haven't heard anything lately from Jim Duff & Company?"

"Not a word," Reade replied. "I don't believe we're yet through with Rough-house camp, however. They're waiting only until our suspicions are allayed. Once in a while we lose one of our workmen to the enemy, and then we have to discharge the poor fellow. Some of our former men have gone away, but there are about thirty of them left in Paloma, and I imagine that they're ready to be ugly when the chance comes. The agent of the Colthwaite Company is still in Paloma. He has been here ever since we came."

"Agent of the Colthwaite Company?" repeated the general manager, opening his eyes. "What's his name?"

"Fred Ransom," Tom replied half carelessly.

"Ransom? Fred Ransom? I never heard of any Colthwaite agent of that name."

"He's one of the Colthwaite people's troublemakers," Tom went on, opening his own eyes rather wide.

"If you were sure of this why didn't you report it to me earlier?"

"Why, I supposed your railroad detectives knew all about it. And that you had heard of it long ago," Reade declared.

"I haven't heard a word of it," continued Mr. Ellsworth, coming down the steps of his car and standing on the ground once more. "What proof have you of Ransom's business here?"

"None whatever," Tom answered cheerfully, "but I had him spotted the first time I heard him talking. He was too entirely positive that we'd fail."

"That was no proof against him."

"No; but Ransom was also certain that the Colthwaite plan was the only one that could bring the Man-killer to time."

"Have you any other reason to suspect this main?" queried Mr. Ellsworth.

"Only the fact that Ransom and Jim Duff have been close friends."

"Where does Ransom stop?"

"At the Mansion House. He has a suite of rooms there, and entertains some kinds of people, including Duff, very lavishly."

"Keep your eyes on that crowd as much as possible, Reade," directed the general manager thoughtfully, as he once more climbed to the platform of his car.

"I will, sir; and it might not be a bad idea to have your detectives do something of the sort, also."

The general manager did not answer, except by a vague nod as his train pulled out from the outskirts of the railway camp.

Tom went back, called for his horse and rode to the westward for another look at the Man-killer. He found Harry, also in saddle, beneath the scanty shade of a struggling tree. Hazelton's quick eyes were taking in every detail of the work being done by the several large gangs of workmen.

"Tom, if we're away from here by Christmas, there's one present you needn't make me," smiled Hazelton wanly, as he caught sight of the camera hanging in its leather field case at his chum's side.

"What present is that?" Tom inquired.

"Don't make me a present of a photograph of this awful place. It's photographed on my brain now, and burned in and baked there. If we ever get through with the Man-killer, and get our money, I never want to see this spot again."

"I'm not thinking at all of the money," Reade retorted lightly yet seriously. "I don't care about the money at present. Nothing will ever satisfy me in life again until I've beaten the Man-killer fairly and squarely. It's the one thing I think about by day and dream of at night."

"I know it," sighed Harry half pityingly.

"Well, what else should we think about?" Tom demanded in a low voice. "Harry, we have the very job, the identical problem, that has thrown down nearly a dozen engineers of fine reputation. Why, boy, this place may be out on the blazing desert, and there may be a dozen discouragements every hour, but we've the finest chance, the biggest unsolved problem in engineering that we could possibly have. It's glorious."

Tom's eyes glowed.

"Go away," grinned Hazelton mischievously, "or I'll catch some of your enthusiasm."

"You don't need any of it," Reade retorted laughingly. "You've tons of enthusiasm stowed away for future use. You know you have."

"I suppose I have enough enthusiasm," Harry admitted, "but I should like to do some actual work. I ride out on the sands every day and sit looking on while the real work is being done. This problem of conquering the Man-killer is growing monotonous. I'm tired of pegging away at the same old task day in and day out."

"Not quite as bad as that," Tom declared. "There's always something a bit new. If you want work to do right now, ride over and show those teamsters where you want them to put the logs that they're bringing up."

This was far too little to satisfy Harry's longing for "doing things," but with a grunt he turned his horse's head and jogged away at a trot.

Tom moved in under the shade of the tree.

"Harry doesn't know enough to appreciate a good thing when he has it," softly laughed Tom, grateful for the scant bit of shade. "Neither does he yet know that often times the brain works best when the body is at rest."

Just then Tom heard a sudden shout from the distance, followed by a chorus of excited voices.

Instantly the young engineer's gaze turned toward the lately filled-in edge of the big sink.

A hundred feet beyond the light platform where some laborers had been working Reade beheld only the head and shoulders of one of the workmen.

"The foolish fellow—to go out so far beyond where the men are allowed to go!" gasped the young chief engineer, setting spurs to his horse.

In a few moments Tom had reached the edge of the sink.

"A rope!" he shouted, and seized the thirty-foot lariat that was handed him. With this, Tom, now on foot, ran within casting distance of the unfortunate, who was being rapidly enveloped by the quicksand.

"Come back, Mr. Reade!" bellowed Foreman Payson. "The drift is setting in on this side of you. Back, like lightning, or you're a doomed man! You'll be swallowed up by the Man-killer yourself!"

But Tom, intent only on saving the unfortunate laborer beyond, was wholly heedless of the fact that his own life was in as great danger.

CHAPTER X. HARRY FIGHTS FOR COMMAND

"Come back, Mr. Reade!" implored Foreman Payson.

For Tom, who had made two casts with the lariat and failed, was knee-deep in shifting sand himself.

"Keep cool!" the young chief engineer called over his shoulder. "I'll be back—both of us in a minute or two."

43

The hapless laborer was now engulfed to his neck in the quicksand.

"Save me! In Heaven's name get me out of this!" begged the poor fellow, frenzied by dread of his seemingly sure fate.

"I'm doing the best I can, friend!" Tom called, as he made a fresh cast.

This time the noose of the raw-hide lariat dropped over the laborer's head.

"Fight your hands free, man!" Tom called encouragingly. "Fight your hands and chest free, so that you can slip the noose down under your armpits. Keep cool and work fast, and we'll have you out. Don't let yourself get excited."

In the meantime Tom was wholly unaware that the engulfing quicksand was reaching up gradually toward his hips.

Foreman Payson had ceased to try to attract Tom's attention. Whatever was to be done to save the chief engineer must be done swiftly. There was not another lariat, or any kind of rope at hand.

Behind was a cloud of alkali dust. Harry Hazelton was riding as fast as he could urge a spirited horse.

In another moment Hazelton had reined up at the edge of the group, dismounting and tossing the reins to one of the workmen.

"My man, you get on that horse and fly for a rope!" ordered Harry.

This last Hazelton shot back over his shoulder, for he was pushing his way through the rapidly forming crowd to Payson's side. Another foreman had just come up.

"Mr. Bell," shouted Harry, "drive the men back who are not needed. We don't want to put a lot of weight on the soil here and cause a further cave-in."

By this time Harry was at the edge of the platform. In a twinkling he was out on the sand.

Grip! Mr. Payson had a strong hold on the collar of the assistant engineer.

"Let go of me!" commanded Harry.

"You can't go out there, Mr. Hazelton. No more lives are to be wasted."

"Let go of me, I tell you!"

"No, sir!" insisted Foreman Payson firmly.

"Let go of me, or I'll fight you!"

"You'll have to fight, then," retorted Payson doggedly, maintaining his grip on the lad's coat collar. "Comeback here!"

Aided by another man, the foreman dragged Hazelton back to the platform.

"Payson, I'll discharge you, if you interfere with me!" stormed Hazelton.

"Don't be a fool, sir. You can't help Mr. Reade. Be cool, sir. Keep your head and direct us like a man of sense."

"Be a man of sense, and see my chum going under the sands of the Man-killer?" flared Hazelton.

He made a bound, doubling his fists threateningly. Then three or four men, at a sign from Payson, seized the young assistant engineer and threw him to the ground.

"Tom," called Harry, "order these fools to let me go."

Reade, however, who had just pulled in all the slack of the rawhide lariat, and had made it fast about his own left arm, seemed wholly unaware of his own great peril.

Tom Reade was now submerged to his waistline in the engulfing sand.

Unless rescued within five minutes the young chief engineer was plainly doomed to be swallowed up in the treacherous sands of the Man-killer. Only a few seconds below the shifting level of the sand would be enough to smother the life out of him. Scores of strong men, powerless to help, watched hopelessly within a few yards of the two whose lives were being slowly but surely snuffed out.

The laborer, whose carelessness or ignorance had caused all the trouble, was now in the sand up to his mouth. The agonized watchers could see him gradually sinking further.

"Keep up your nerve, friend!" called Tom, in cool encouragement. "We'll soon have you out of that."

Gripping the lariat with both bands, Tom gave a strong, sudden wrench and succeeded in drawing the imperiled man out of the sand a few inches.

Then the poor fellow began to settle again moaning piteously as he saw a hideous death staring him in the face.

Tom Reade's own face was deathly white from a realization of the other's peril. Of his own danger the young chief engineer had not once stopped to think.

Harry Hazelton was again on his feet. That much Foreman Payson had permitted, but strong-armed laborers stood on either side of the boy, and their detaining grips were on his arm.

Out yonder the doomed man saw the engulfing sand creeping up on a level with his eyes. He tried to scream, but the sand shifted into his mouth. In pitiable terror the poor fellow closed his mouth in order to delay death for another moment. Even to call for help would now be swiftly fatal!

Behind came the thunder of hoofs.

"Ropes!" shouted the horseman on Harry's mount.

He rode past the groups of men, close to the platform. Then, leaping from the saddle, the rider tossed a small bundle of ropes at Harry's feet. All were ropes and lines—not a raw-hide among them.

"There he goes! He's gone!" roared a score of frantic voices, as the engulfed laborer sank out of sight in the sand.

Harry Hazelton feverishly uncoiled one of the ropes, gathering a few folds in his right hand.

"Catch, Tom!" Harry shouted, making a cast.

The line swirled through the air, then settled on the sands.

"O-o-o-oh!" groaned Hazelton, for the rope had fallen four feet to one side of Reade, and the latter, hemmed in as he was, could not reach it.

"Take your time and make a sure throw, Harry!" Tom called cheerily.

Again Hazelton made a throw—and failed.

"Let me, have that! My head's cooler," called Foreman Payson.

He made two quick, steady throws, but each shot wide of the mark.

"Let me have that!" screamed Harry, snatching the line away.

"There are lines enough. Two men might be making throws," spoke a quiet voice behind them.

Payson nodded, and bent over for another line.

All trace of the doomed laborer had now disappeared. As for Tom, the sand was reaching up under his arm-pits. The young chief engineer had had the presence of mind to keep his arms free, but soon they too must be swallowed up.

"Good throw—whoever sent it!" cheered Tom Reade, as a final cast— Harry's—sent a line within six inches of his face.

Tom could not see those back at the platform, for his back was turned to the eastward, and he could no longer swing his body about.

"Get it under your arms-quick, Tom, or you're done for, too!" screamed Harry.

"Keep cool, old chap!" came back the unconcerned answer. "It isn't half bad out here. The sand feels really cool about one's body."

"This is no time for nonsense!" ordered Hazelton hoarsely. "Have you the line fast?"

"Yes!" nodded Reade. "Haul away! Careful, but strong and steady!"

Under Foreman Payson's direction a score of men seized the other end of the line and then began to haul.

Harry danced up and down in a frenzy.

"Tom, you idiot," he gasped. "You haven't made the line fast about yourself."

"Not yet," came the cheery answer. "That wouldn't be fair play. Haul away on our friend out yonder."

Tom Reade had knotted the line fast to his end of the rawhide lariat that was tied under the shoulders of the engulfed laborer. It was magnificent, though seemingly a useless sacrifice of his own life for one who must already be dead.

From some of the workmen a faint cheer went up as the slowly incoming line hauled the head of the unconscious laborer above the sand. A foot at a time the body came toward them over the sand.

Harry, however, scarcely noted the rescue. He was frantically working with another line, knotting it in a sort of harness under his own shoulders.

"Come here, some of you men!" he called. "Bear a hand here! Lively!"

Foreman Payson was instantly at the side of the young assistant engineer.

"What are you trying to do, Mr. Hazelton?" he demanded.

"I'm going out on the sands," retorted Harry. "I'm going to reach Tom Reade. If I go under the men can aid me."

"But that isn't a rawhide line; it's hemp," objected Foreman Payson.

"It's strong enough," retorted Hazelton impatiently.

"I don't know about that."

"It will have to do," insisted Hazelton. "You men get a good hold. Also, one of you play out this other line that I'm taking with me for Tom Reade."

"Don't risk anything foolish, Harry!" called the voice of Tom Reade, who now felt the sand under his chin.

"I'm coming to you," Tom, shouted Harry.

"It's too dangerous. Don't!"

"I've got to come to you!"

"I tell you don't! Maybe I can get myself out."

"Yes, you can," jeered Hazelton. "Tom, if you went under, do you think I could ever go back to our native town?"

"Payson!" shouted Tom.

"Yes, sir!"

"Don't let Mr. Hazelton come—yet. Seize him!"

"I've got him, sir!"

Harry felt himself seized by the strong arms of the foreman.

"You don't go, sir," Payson insisted. "It's a criminal waste of life."

"Man, unhand me. Let me go, I tell you."

"I won't, sir. I've Mr. Reade's orders."

"He's helpless and no longer in command," Harry retorted.

"He's in command enough for me, sir."

"Payson!" Harry Hazelton's fierce gaze burned into the eyes of the foreman. "If Tom Reade dies out yonder, and you've hindered me from saving him—I'll have your life for forfeit!"

Before that burning look even Payson shrank back. Harry Hazelton, ordinarily the best natured of boys, was now in terrible earnest.

"That's right," muttered Hazelton. "Men, I take command here. You needn't heed any words from Reade. Now, you men on the lines watch close and listen keenly for my orders."

With that Hazelton darted out on the deadly, treacherous sands!

CHAPTER XI. CHEATING THE MAN-KILLER

For the first few yards the assistant engineer ran almost as well as though on a cinder track. Then his feet sank in. Soon he stumbled.

Then there came a time, within ten feet of Tom, when Harry felt his feet settling in the sand despite his efforts to pull himself out.

In the meantime the haulers on the other line had forgotten to pull the laborer nearer to safety.

"You men get your eyes on the job!" sternly commanded Payson, who seemed capable of having eyes everywhere.

Harry got out, somehow. He made a bound, landing within arm's length of Tom Reade.

"I'm here, old chum!" gasped Hazelton.

"I knew you'd be," returned Tom calmly, "if there were any way of doing it."

Harry pulled himself together and floundered still closer.

Nor was there a moment to be lost. Tom was already reduced to the choice between silence and having his mouth filled with sand.

Harry's hands worked with lightning speed. Feverishly he dug out the sand, until he had scooped away enough to bare Tom's shoulders and a few inches beneath.

Swoop! Down went the extra noose over Tom's lifted arms, and then down to a snug noose under his armpits.

From the platform a cheer went up, for the unconscious laborer had just been hauled to safety.

It was with a thrill of horror that Hazelton found his own legs firmly embedded in the sand well up to his thighs.

"Get Reade started first!" shouted the young assistant engineer. "Don't bother with me until I give the word."

How the line fastened to Tom tightened and strained! At times it seemed as though it must give way.

Presently Tom's shoulder and a part of his torso were free.

In the meantime Harry Hazelton had sunk in up to the waist line.

"We'll haul on you, too, now, Mr. Hazelton!" sounded the voice of Foreman Payson.

"Don't you dare do it until I give the word," thundered back the voice of the assistant engineer.

With a line securely about him, Harry felt that he could afford to take the slight chance of waiting his turn.

He saw Tom's knees coming up out of the sand before he called:

"Now, Payson, you can give me a little boost if you like. Don't pull me in ahead of Tom Reade, however."

Presently deafening cheers went up. Both young engineers were being slowly, surely hauled to safe ground.

Then Tom and Harry reached a spot where they could rise to their own feet and floundered. Tom started, then swayed dizzily.

"Steady, there, old Gridley boy!" mumbled Hazelton, slipping an arm around his recovered chum.

Then the two young engineers reached the platform and a fresh tumult of joyful cheering burst forth.

"Payson," exclaimed Harry, going up to the foreman, and holding out his hand, "will you accept my apologies for all I said to you? I had to use strong language, or you'd have held me back from Reade."

"I didn't believe he could be saved," returned the foreman, with a sickly smile, as he grasped Hazelton's outstretched hand.

Tom, too weak at first to stand, had dropped to his knees at the side of the unconscious laborer, over whom some of the bystanders were working in stupid fashion.

"This man must have medical attention at once!" Tom declared. "Some of you men lift him to your shoulders. Be careful not to jolt him, but travel at a jog all the way to the office building. Harry, can you sit on your horse?"

"Surely," said the young assistant.

"Lucky boy, then," smiled Reade. "I won't be able to sit in saddle for some minutes. Ride into camp and tell the operator to wire swiftly for a physician to come out and attend to that man."

"But you—"

"I'm here, am I not!" smiled Reade.

"I should say you are, Mr. Reade!" came a hoarse, friendly roar from one of the laborers.

Hazelton did not delay. He was soon speeding back over the desert.

As for Tom, there were many offers of assistance, but he explained that all he needed was to keep quiet and have a chance to get his breath back.

Payson, in the meantime, had started the work going again, though most of his men toiled with far less spirit than before the accident.

Ten minutes later Tom mounted his horse and rode slowly back toward camp. By the time he reached there he made out the automobile of a Paloma physician coming in haste.

Tom was still weak enough to tremble as Harry stepped outside and helped him to the ground.

"Harry," Reade remarked dryly, "I'm not going to bother to thank you for such a simple little thing as saving my life out yonder. I am well aware that you had the time of your life in doing it."

"I might have had the time of my life," returned Harry, with an imitation of his chum's calmness, "if there had been more excitement about it. It was all rather dull, wasn't it, old chap?"

Smiling, both stepped inside. Then Tom's face became grave when he saw that the rescued laborer had not yet recovered consciousness.

"Somewhere in the world," murmured Reade, as he dropped to one knee and rested a finger-tip on the laborer's pulse, "there's someone—a woman, or a child, or a white-haired old man—who wouldn't wish us to let this man die. What have you men been doing for him?"

Before the answer could be given a honk sounded at the door. Then a young doctor clad in white duck and carrying a three-fold medicine case, stepped inside.

"Sucked down by the sand and hauled out again, Doc," Tom explained.

The physician looked closely at his patient and Harry drove out the men who had no especial business there.

"A little pin-head of glonoin on his tongue for a beginning," decided the physician, opening his case. From one of the vials he took a small pellet, forcing it between the lips of the unconscious man. Then, with his stethoscope, he listened for the heart beats.

"Another glonoin, and then we'll start in to wake up our friend," said the young doctor in white duck, after a pause.

Two or three minutes later the laborer opened his eyes.

"You've been trying not to hear the whistle," laughed the doctor gently. "A big fellow like you must be up and doing."

Ten minutes later the doctor found Tom outside.

"The man will be all right now, with a little stuff that I'll leave for him," smiled the visitor. "Of course there's some man in camp who can look after a comrade to-night?"

"Doc, couldn't you do a better job if you had the man in Paloma under your own eyes tonight?" Tom questioned.

"Yes; undoubtedly."

"Can you take him?"

"Yes."

"Then do so. Give him all the attention he needs. Make out your bill to the A. G. & N. M. Hand it to me, and I'll O.K. it and send it in to headquarters for payment. If you think an automobile ride after dark will do the poor chap good, give him one and put that in your bill, too."

"Reade, I want to shake hands with you," said the physician earnestly. "I've looked after railroad hands before, but this is the first time I was ever asked to be humane to one. Have no fear but I'll send this man back to you strong and grateful. What's his name?"

"I don't know," returned Reade. "I don't even know to whose gang he belongs, though I think he's one of Payson's men."

Late the following afternoon the laborer was brought back to camp. The following morning he returned to his work as usual.

During the next two weeks Tom and Harry directed all their energies, as well as the labor of all of their men, to bridging over that bad spot in the Man-killer that had so nearly claimed two lives. One after another six different layers of log network were put down. The open box cars brought up thousands of tons of good soil, which was dumped down into the layers of interlaced logs.

"The old Man-killer must feel tremendously flattered at finding himself so persistently manicured," laughed Tom as he sat in saddle watching the men putting down the sixth layer.

Steel piles, hollow and filled with cement, were being driven here, the cement not going in until the top of the pile was but four feet above the level of the desert.

"Look out yonder," nodded Harry, handing his field glass to his chum. "You can just make out a glint on the sand. That's one of our steel piles being sucked under."

"The explorer of a few centuries hence may find a lot of these piles," laughed Tom. "If he does, he'll most likely attribute them to the Pueblo Indians or the Aztecs, and he'll write a learned volume about the high state of civilization that existed among the savages here before the white man came."

"I'm mighty glad, Tom, that General Manager Ellsworth isn't out here to see how many dozens of steel piles we're feeding hopelessly to the Man-killer."

"Not one of those piles is going down hopelessly," Tom retorted. "Some of the piles may disappear, and never be seen again, but each one will help hold the drift at some point, near the surface, or perhaps a thousand feet below the surface."

"Only a thousand feet below the surface!" Harry grunted. "Tom, I often feel certain that the Man-killer extends away down to the center of the earth and up again on the other side. Before I'm a very old man I expect to hear that several of our steel piles have shot up above the surface in China or India."

Hearing the noise of horse's hoofs behind him, Tom turned. He beheld Fred Ransom riding out to the spot on a mottled "calico" horse.

"Look who's here," Reade murmured to his chum.

"What are you going to do with him?" asked Hazelton, after a quick look. "Run him off the line?"

"I don't know," Tom answered slowly. "Ransom is trying hard to earn a living, you know."

Harry snorted. That sort of estimation of Ransom, even as a joke, was a little too much for him.

"Mighty hot day, Reade," called Ransom, as he reined in near the young engineers.

"Yes," said Tom slowly. "If I were enjoying myself beside a bottle of cold soda on the Mansion House porch I don't believe I'd have the energy to call for a horse and ride all the way out here in the heat."

"Am I intruding?" demanded Ransom, with a swift, keen glance at the young chief engineer.

"Oh, no, indeed!" came Tom's response. "You're as welcome as the flowers in spring."

"Thank you. It's a fine job you're doing out here."

"Now it's my turn to extend my thanks to you," Tom drawled. "Your praise is all the more appreciated as coming from a competitor."

"A competitor!" asked Ransom quickly, and with a half scowl. "I'm not an engineer."

"Your people are ranked as pretty fair engineers," Reade rejoined.

"My people? What do you mean, Reade? There isn't an engineer in our family."

"No; but the Colthwaite Company employs a good many engineers," Tom suggested.

"Colthwaite?" repeated Ransom, now on his guard. "I have nothing to do with that concern."

"No?" asked Tom, as though greatly astonished. "Why, that's strange."

"Why is it strange?"

"Why," Tom Reade rejoined amiably, "everyone connected with the A. G. & N. M. who knows anything at all about you credits you with being a member of the Colthwaite Company's gloom department."

"Gloom department?" gasped Ransom, with a wholly innocent-looking face. "Oh, all right. I'll bite. What is a gloom department, anyway?"

"It's a comparatively recent piece of business apparatus," smiled Tom. "It is employed by big corporations as a club with which to hit smaller crowds that want some of the business of life. The gloom department might be called the bureau of knocking, or the hit-in-the-neck shift."

"Is that what you accuse me of doing for the Colthwaite Company?" asked Fred Ransom, his scowl deepening.

"Oh, the accusation isn't all mine," Tom assured him unconcernedly. "Some of it belongs elsewhere."

"Your suspicions are utterly unwarranted," retorted Ransom, choking slightly.

"It's a lot of comfort to hear you say so," Tom rejoined, as smilingly as ever.

"You're on the wrong track this time, anyway," Ransom asserted boldly. "Still, I don't suppose you want me out here."

"On the contrary, I greatly enjoy seeing you here," Tom declared. "I'm very grateful for the praise you offered me a moment ago."

"You're welcome," returned the Colthwaite agent, trying hard to smile. "However, I won't take up your time. Good afternoon."

"Good afternoon, then," nodded Tom. "Drop in again, won't you? Any time within working hours."

"Confound that fellow Reade!" muttered Ransom angrily as he rode back to Paloma. "He knows altogether too much—or suspects it. I shall have to call Jim Duff's attention to him!"

"Why did you string the fellow so?" asked Harry when the chums were alone once more.

"I didn't," Reade retorted. "I came very close to giving him straight information."

"Now he'll be more on his guard."

"That won't do him any good," Tom yawned. "He has been on his guard all along, yet we found him out. For that matter, any man who lives regularly at the Mansion House these days is open to our suspicion."

For the Mansion House, ever since Tom's having been ordered away, had been a losing proposition. Now and then a traveling salesman stopped there, though not many.

"By the way, Harry," predicted Tom, as the chums were riding back to Paloma at the close of the afternoon, "look out, in about three of four days, for a new and permanent guest at the Cactus House."

"Who's coming?" inquired Hazelton.

"Whatever man the Colthwaite Company decides to send to the Cactus House as soon as headquarters in Chicago receives Ransom's report. I think we'll know that new chap, too, when he shows up. Also, you'll find that the new man is either an avowed enemy of Ransom, after a little, or else he won't choose to know Ransom at all."

"That's pretty wild guessing," scoffed Harry Hazelton.

"Wait three or four days, and see whether it's guessing or one of the fine fruits of logic," proposed Reade. "Incidentally, the Colthwaite people will wonder why it didn't occur to them before to send one of their gloom men to live at the Cactus. Fact is, I've been looking for the chap for more than a fort-night."

CHAPTER XII. HOW THE TRAP WAS BAITED

It was the evening of the day after Harry, who had insisted on trudging up and down the line all day, instead of using his horse, had a touch of heat headache.

He was not in a serious condition, but he needed rest. He dropped into one of the chairs on the Cactus House porch and prepared to doze.

"Is there anything I can get for you, or do for you, old chap?" inquired Tom, coming out on the porch after supper and looking remarkably comfortable and contented.

"No; just let me doze," begged Harry. "I feel a trifle drowsy."

"Then, if you're going to give a concert through your nose," smiled Tom, "I may as well protect myself by going some distance away."

"Go along."

"I believe I'll take a walk. Probably, too, the ice cream man will be richer when I get back."

Tom went down into the street and sauntered along. He had walked but a few blocks when he met another young man in white ducks.

"Doc, I'm looking for the place where the ice cream flows," Reade hinted. "Can I tempt you?"

"Without half trying," laughed Dr. Furniss the young physician who had gone out to camp to attend the Man-killer victim.

As they were seated together over their ice cream, Dr. Furniss inquired:

"By the way, do you ever see my one-time patient nowadays?"

"The fellow we exhumed from the Man-killer?"

"The same."

"I see him every morning," laughed Tom. "Really, I can't help seeing him, for the man puts himself in my way daily to say good morning. And as yet I haven't learned his name."

"His name is Tim Griggs," replied Dr. Furniss. "He's a fine fellow, too, in his rough, manly way. He's wonderfully grateful to you, Reade. Do you know why?"

"Haven't an idea."

"Well, Tim's sheet anchor in life is a little girl."

"Sweetheart?"

"After a fashion," laughed the young doctor. "The girl is his daughter, eight years old. She's everything to Tim, for his wife is dead. The child lives with somewhat distant relatives, in a New England town. Tim sends all his spare money to her, and so the child is probably well looked after. Tim told me, with a big choke in his voice, that, if the Man-killer had swallowed him up, it would have been all up with the little girl, too. When money stopped coming the relatives would probably have set the child to being household drudge for the family. Tim has a round dozen of different photos of the child taken at various times."

"Then I'm extra glad we got him out of the Man-killer," said Tom rather huskily.

"I knew you'd be glad, Reade. You're that kind of fellow."

"Tim Griggs, then, is probably one of our steady men," Tom remarked, after a while.

"Steady! Why the man generally sends all of his month's pay, except about eight dollars, to his daughter. From what he tells me she is a sharp, thrifty little thing. She pays her own board bill with her relatives, chooses and pays for her own clothes, and puts the balance of the money in bank for herself and her father."

"Does Tim ever go to see her?"

"Once in two years, regularly. He'd go east oftener, but it costs too much money. He'd live near her, but he says he can earn more money down here on the desert. Tim even talks about a college education for that idolized girl. She looks out just as sharply for her daddy. Whenever Tim is ready to make a trip east, she sends him the money for his fare. The two have a great old time together."

"Tim may marry again one of these days, and then the young lady may not have as happy a time," remarked Tom thoughtfully.

"I hinted as much to Griggs," replied Dr. Furniss, "but he told me, pretty strongly, that there'll be no new wife for him until he has helped the daughter to find her own place in life."

"Say!" muttered Tom, with a queer little choke in his voice. "The heroes in life generally aren't found on the high spots, are they?"

"They're not," retorted the doctor solemnly.

Half an hour later, after having eaten their fill of ice cream, Dr. Furniss and Engineer Reade parted, Tom strolling on alone in the darkness.

"I can It get that fellow Griggs out of my mind," muttered Tom. "To think that a splendid fellow like him is working as a laborer! I wonder if he isn't fitted for something better—something that pays better? Look out, Tom Reade, you old softy, or you'll be doing something foolish, all on account of a primary school girl in New England whom you've never seen, and never will! I wonder—hello!"

As Tom had walked along his head had sunk lower and lower in thought. His sudden exclamation had been brought forth by the fact that he had bumped violently into another human being.

"Cantch er look out where you're going?" demanded an ugly voice.

"I should have been looking out, my friend," Tom replied amiably. "It was very careless of me. I trust, that I haven't done you serious harm."

"Quit yer sass!" ordered the other, who was a tall, broad-shouldered and very surly looking fellow of thirty.

"I don't much blame you for being peevish," Reade went on. "Still, I think there has been no serious harm done. Good night, friend."

"No, ye don't!" snarled the other. "Nothing of the slip-away-easy style, like that!"

"Why, what do you want?" I asked Tom, opening his eyes in genuine surprise.

"Ye thick-headed idiot!" rasped the surly stranger. "Ye—"

From that the stranger launched into a strain of abuse that staggered the young engineer.

"Say no more," begged Reade generously. "I accept your apology, just as you've phrased it."

"Apology, ye fool!" growled the stranger.

"That won't do. Put up your hands!"

"Why?"

"So ye can fight, ye—"

"Fight?" echoed Tom, with a shake of his bead. "On a hot night like this? No, sir! I refuse."

Tom would have passed peaceably on his way, but the stranger suddenly let go a terrific right-hander. Had Tom Reade received the blow he would have gone to the ground. But the young engineer's athletic training stood by him. He slid out, easily and gracefully, but was compelled to wheel and face his assailant.

"Don't," urged Tom. "It's too hot."

"I'm hot myself," leered the stranger, dancing nearer.

"You look it," Tom admitted. "If you don't stop dancing, you'll soon be hotter. It makes me warm to look at you."

"Stop this one, ye tin-horn!" snarled the stranger.

"Certainly," agreed Tom, blocking the blow. "However, I wish you wouldn't be so strenuous. One of us may get hurt."

This last escaped Reade as he blocked the blow, and again displayed a neat little bit of footwork.

"Let's see you stop this one!" taunted the bully.

"Certainly," agreed Tom, and did so.

"And this one. And this! Here's another!"

By this time the blows were raining in fast and thick. Tom's agile footwork kept him out of reach of the hard, hammer-like fists of the stranger.

Tom had been bred in athletics. He was comparative master of boxing, but before this interchange of blows had gone far the young engineer realized that he had met a doughty opponent.

What Tom didn't know was that his present foe was an ex-prizefighter, who had sunk low in the scale of life.

What the lad didn't even suspect was that the man had been hired to pick a fight with him, and that the fight was for desperate stakes.

"Have you pounded me all you think necessary?" asked Tom coolly, after more than a minute's hard interchange of blows in which neither man had gained any notable advantage.

"No, ye slant-eared boob!" roared the assailant. "Ye—"

Here he launched into another stream of abuse.

"You said all that before," remarked Tom, with a new flash in his eyes. Then fully aroused, he went to work in earnest, intending to drive his opponent back and down him.

The fighting became terrific. There was little effort now to parry, for each fighter had become intent on bringing the other to earth.

Tom was soon panting as he fought, for his opponent was heavier, taller and altogether out of the youth's fistic class.

"If I can only reach his wind once, and topple him over!" thought Reade.

A blow aimed at his jaw he failed to block. The impact sent the young engineer half staggering. Another blow, and Tom dropped, knocked out.

At that very instant a street door near by opened noiselessly.

"I've got him," leered the bully, bending over the senseless form of Tom Reade.

"Bring him in!" ordered a voice behind the open doorway.

CHAPTER XIII. TOM HEARS THE PROGRAM

Throwing his arms around Tom, the bully lifted him and bore him inside, dropping him on the floor in the dark.

"He's some tough fighter," muttered Tom's assailant. "I didn't know but he'd get me."

"No; he couldn't," replied the other voice. "I was just opening the door so I could slip out and give him a clip in the dark."

"He's coming to," muttered the bully. "Ye'll have to tell me what you want done with him."

The speaker had knelt by Tom, with a hand roughly laid against the young engineer's pulse. Neither plotter could see the boy, for no light had been struck in the room.

"Pick him up," ordered the one who appeared to be directing affairs. "If he comes to while you're carrying him you can handle him easily enough, can't you?"

"Of course. Even after he knows pie from dirt he'll be dazed for a few minutes."

"Come along with him."

"Strike a light."

For answer the director of this brutal affair flashed a little glow from a pocket electric lamp.

The way led down a hallway, through to the back of the house, and thence down a steep flight of stairs into a cellar.

The man who appeared to be in charge of this undertaking had brought a lantern, holding it ahead of the man who carried Tom's unconscious form.

"Dump him there," ordered the man with the lantern.

"He's stirring," reported the fighter, after having dropped young Reade to the hard earthen floor.

"Take this then," replied the other, who, having hung the lantern on a hook overhead, had stepped off beyond the fringe of darkness. He now returned with a shotgun, which he handed to the fighter who had attacked the young chief engineer in the street.

"Do you want me to shoot him?" whispered the other huskily.

"If you have to, but I don't believe it will be necessary. The cub will soon understand that his safety depends entirely on doing as he is told."

"Say," muttered Tom thickly. He stirred, opened his eyes, then sat up, looking dazed.

"Don't move or talk too much," advised the man with the shotgun. As he spoke, he moved the muzzle close to Reade's face.

"Hello!" muttered Tom, blinking rather hard.

"Hello yourself. That's talking enough for you to do," snapped the bully.

"Was that the thing you hit me over the head with at the finish?" inquired the young engineer curiously.

"Careful! You're expected to think—not talk," leered his captor. "If ye want something to think about ye can remember that I have fingers on both triggers of this gun."

"I can see that much," Tom assented. "Why do you think that it's necessary to keep that thing pointed at me? Have you got me in a place where you feel that facilities for escaping are too great?"

The word "facilities" appeared too big for the mind of the bully to grasp.

"I don't know what ye're talkin' about," he grumbled.

"Neither do I," Tom admitted cheerily. "My friend, I'm not going to irritate you by pretending that I know more than you do. In fact, I know less, for I have no idea what is about to happen to me here, and that's something that you do know."

"No; I don't," glared his captor, "and I don't care what is going to happen to you."

Back of the fringe between light and darkness steps were heard on the cellar stairs. Then someone moved steadily forward until he came into the light.

"Hello, Jim!" Tom called good-humoredly.

"Don't try to be too familiar with your betters, young man!" came the stern reply.

"Oh, a thousand pardons, Mr. Duff," Tom amended hastily. "I didn't intend to insult your dignity. Indeed, I am only too glad to find you resolved to be dignified."

"If you try to get fresh with me," growled the gambler, "I'll knock your head off."

"Call it a slap on the wrist, and let it go at that," urged Tom. "I'm very nervous to-night, and a blow on the head might make me worse."

"Nothing could make you worse," growled, Duff, turning on his heel, "and only death could improve you."

"Then I'm distinctly opposed to the up-lift," grinned Tom, but Duff had disappeared into a darker part of the cellar and the young engineer could not tell whether or not his shaft had reached its mark.

"Ye wouldn't be so fresh if ye had a good idea of what ye're up against to-night," warned the bully with the gun.

"I fancy a good many of us would tone down if we could look ahead for three whole days," Tom suggested.

Other steps were now heard on the stairs. The newcomers remained outside the illuminated part of the cellar until still others arrived.

"Now, gentlemen," proposed the voice of Jim Duff, "suppose we have a look at the troublemaker."

"They can't mean me," Tom hinted to his immediate captor.

"Shut up!" came the surly answer.

Fully a dozen men now moved forward. With the single exception of Duff, each had a cloth, with eye-holes, tied in place over his face.

"My, but this looks delightfully mysterious!" chuckled Tom.

"You be still, boy, except when you answer something that calls for a reply," ordered Jim Duff, who had dropped all of the surface polish of manner that he usually employed. "This meeting need not last long, and I'll do most of the talking."

"Won't these other gentlemen present be allowed to do some of the talking?" the young engineer inquired.

"They don't want to," Duff explained gruffly. "That might lead to their being recognized."

"Oh, that's the game?" mused Tom Reade aloud. "Why, I thought they had the handkerchiefs over their faces because—"

"Shut up and listen!" warned Jim Duff.

"...because," finished Tom, "they wanted me to feel that everything was being done regularly and in good dime-novel form. My, but they do look like some of the fellows that Hen Dutcher used to tell us about. Hen used to waste more time on dime novels than—"

"Shut up!" again commanded Duff. "These gentlemen feel that there is no need of their being recognized."

"Then why didn't Fred Ransom, of the Colthwaite Company, cover up the scar on his chin?" retorted Reade. "Why didn't Ashby, of the Mansion House, invent a new style of walking for the occasion?"

Both men named drew hastily back into the shadow. Tom chuckled quietly.

"I could name a few others," Tom continued carelessly. "In fact—I think I know you all. Gentlemen, you might as well remove your masks."

"Club him with the butt of the gun, if he talks too much," Duff directed the bully, who had stepped back a few paces as the men formed a circle around the young engineer.

"Did you ever try to stop water from running down hill, Duff," Tom inquired good-humoredly.

"What has that to do with—" began the gambler angrily.

"Nothing very much," Tom admitted. "Only it's a waste of time to try to bind my tongue. The only thing you can do is to gag me; but, from some things you've let drop, I judge that you want me to do some of the talking presently."

"We do," nodded Duff, seeking to regain his temper. "However, it won't do you any good to attempt to do your talking before you've heard me."

"If I've been interfering with your rights, then I certainly owe you an apology," Tom answered, with mock gravity. "May I beg you to begin your speech?"

"I will if you'll keep quiet long enough, boy," Jim Duff retorted.

"I'll try," sighed Reade. "Let's hear you."

"This committee of gentlemen—" began the gambler.

"All gentlemen?" Tom inquired gravely.

"This committee," Duff started again, "have concerned themselves with the fact that you have done much to make business bad here in Paloma. You have prevented hundreds of workmen from coming into Paloma to spend their wages as they otherwise would have done."

"Some mistake there," Reade urged. "I can't control the actions of my men after working hours."

"You've persuaded them against coming into town," retorted Duff sternly. "None of the A. G. & N. M. workmen come into Paloma with their wages."

"I'm glad to hear that," Tom nodded. "It's the effect of taking good advice, not the result of orders."

Some of the masked listeners stirred impatiently.

"It's all the same," Jim growled. "Your men don't come into town, and Paloma suffers from the loss of that much business."

"I'm sorry to hear it."

"So this committee," the gambler went on, "has instructed me to inform you that your immediate departure from Paloma will be necessary if you care to go on living."

"I can't go just yet," Tom declared, with a shake of his bead. "My work here at Paloma isn't finished."

"Your work will be finished before the night is over, if you don't accept our orders to leave town," growled Duff.

"Dear me! Is it as bad as that?" queried Reade.

"Worse, as you'll find! What's your answer, Reade?"

"All I can say then," Tom replied innocently, "is that it is too bad."

Clip! Jim Duff bent forward, administering a smart cuff against the right side of the sitting engineer's face.

"Don't do that!" warned Tom, leaping lithely to his feet. He faced the gambler coolly, but the lad's muscles were working under the sleeves of his shirt.

Duff drew back three steps, after which he faced the boy, eyeing him steadily.

"Reade, you've heard what we have to say to you. That you can't go on living in Paloma. Are you ready to give us your word to leave Paloma before daylight, and never come back?"

"No," Tom replied flatly.

"Then," sneered the gambler, fixing the gaze of his snake-like eyes on the young chief engineer, "I'll tell you what we have provided for you. We shall take you to the edge of the town, at once, and there hang you by the neck to a tree. After you've ceased squirming we'll fasten this card to you."

From another man present Jim snatched a printed card, bearing this legend:
"Gone, for the good of the community!"

CHAPTER XIV. THE COUNCIL OF THE CURB

"How soon are you going to carry out your plans?" Reade demanded.

"Then you won't leave Paloma?"

"I certainly won't—as far as my own decision goes," Reade replied firmly. "Furthermore, I should feel the utmost contempt for myself if I allowed you to drive me away from here before my work is completed."

"You're a fool!" hissed Duff.

"And you're a gambler," Tom shot back. "If you won't change your trade, why should you expect me to change mine?"

"I reckon, gentlemen," said Duff, turning to the others present, "that there's no use in wasting any more time with this fellow. He'd rather be hanged to a tree than take good advice. If the rest of you agree with me, I propose that we take the cub to his tree at once."

Several spoke in favor of this plan. Tom, seeing this, felt his heart sink somewhat within him, though he was no more inclined than before to accede to the demands of the rascals.

"Grab him! Throw him down; tie and gag him," were the gambler's orders.

Two men nearest the young engineer sprang at him.

"We'll play this game right through to the finish, then!" burst from Tom's lips, and there was something like fury in his voice.

Biff! Thump!

Two of the townsmen of Paloma, wholly unprepared for resistance, went down before the engineer's telling blows.

"Your turn, Duff!" rumbled Reade's voice, as he sprang forward and launched a terrific blow at the gambler.

Duff went down, almost doubling up as he struck. He had been hit squarely on the jaw with a force that made even Tom Reade's hardened knuckles ache.

"Shoot him!" rose a snarl, as others moved toward the boy.

"All right!" assented Tom, his voice ringing cheerily despite his anger. "Be cowards, as comes natural to you. Yet, if you have the courage of real men I'll agree to fight my way out of this place, meeting you one at a time."

"What's that noise up in the street?" suddenly demanded Ashby, in a tone of sudden fear.

"Run up and find out, if you want to know," proposed Tom, who stood poised, ready for another assailant to come within reach of his fists.

Stealthily, on tip-toe, the bully who had first engaged Reade in the street fight, was now trying to get up behind the young engineer. The bully held the shotgun ready to bring down on the lad's head.

"There's some row up there," continued Ashby. "There, I heard shots!"

"Brave, aren't you?" jeered Tom.

Three or four of the masked cowards started for the steep stairway.

Even the bully with the clubbed shotgun must have been seized with fear; for, though in position to strike, he quickly lowered the weapon and listened.

Bump! smash! sounded, though not directly overhead.

Then from the hallway above came the noise of the treading of many feet, while a voice roared hoarsely:

"Spread through the house, boys! If they've done anything to Mr. Reade, then break the necks of every white-livered rascal you can find!"

"Fine!" chuckled Tom, while the masked faces in the cellar turned even whiter than the cloths covering them. "That voice sounds familiar to me, too."

Over the hubbub of voices above sounded some remonstrating tones, as though others were urging a less violent course.

"It's the workmen from the camp!" guessed Hotelman Ashby, in a voice that shook as though from ague.

"Sounds like it," chuckled Tom. "Cheer up, Ashby. If it's our railroad crew I'll try to see to it that they don't do more than half kill you!"

Then, raising his voice, Tom called gleefully:

"Hello, there! You'll find us in the cellar."

"Why don't you kill that fool!" muttered Jim Duff, who, still dazed, struggled to sit up.

"Hush, man, for goodness sake!" implored the badly frightened Ashby.

Duff, with rapidly returning consciousness, now leaped to his feet, drawing his pistol and springing at Reade.

"Hold on!" Tom proposed coolly. "You're too late!"

The sudden flooding of light into the place and the rush of hobnailed shoes on the stairs recalled even the gambler's scattered senses.

"There they are!" yelled a voice. "Grab 'em! Be careful you don't hit Mr. Reade."

In another instant the cellar was the center of a wild scene. Railway laborers flooded the little place. While some held dark lanterns that threw a bright glow over the scene, others leaped upon the masked ones, tearing the cloths from their faces.

"Serve 'em hot!" roared the same rough voice.

"Stop!" commanded Tom Reade, leaping forward where the light was brightest and into the thick of the struggling mass of humanity.

"Stop, I tell you!"

His commands fell upon deaf ears. It was impossible to restrain these men.

Here and there the lately masked men drew pistols, though not one of them had a chance to use his weapon ere it was wrested from him.

Pound! slam! bang! A medley of falling blows filled the air, nor was it many seconds later when cries of pain and fear, and appeals for mercy were heard on all sides.

Tom had recognized his own railroad workers, and was throwing himself among them, doing his utmost with hands and voice to stop the brief but wild orgy of revenge on the part of the workmen who idolized him. In their present rage, however, Tom could not at once restrain them. Time and again he was swept back from reaching Tim Griggs, who was easily the center of this volcanic outburst of human passion.

"Boys!" roared Tim. "We'll want to know these coyotes to-morrow. Black the left eye of each rascal. I'll black both of Jim Duff's."

Two heavy, sodden impacts sounded during a brief pause in the noise, attesting to the fact that the gambler had been decorated.

"Stop all this! Stop!" roared Tom Reade. "Men, we're not savages, just because these other fellows happen to be! Stop it, I tell you. Are there no foremen here?"

"I'm trying to reach you, Mr. Reade," called the voice of Superintendent Hawkins. "But this is a heavy crush to get through."

In truth it was. There were more than a hundred laborers in the cellar, while the stairs were blocked by a mob of enraged workmen.

"Stop it all, men!" Tom again urged, and this time there was silence, save for his own strong voice. "We don't want to prove ourselves to be as despicable as the enemy are. Bring 'em up to the street, but don't be brutal about it. We'll look the scoundrels over so that we'll know them to-morrow. Come along. Clear the stairs, if you please, men!"

Tom was now once more in control, as fully as though he had his force of toilers out on the desert at the Man-killer quicksand.

So, after a few minutes, all were in the street. Here fully two hundred more of the railroad men, many of them armed with stakes and other crude weapons, held back a crowd of Paloma residents who swarmed curiously about.

"Let me through, men. Let me through, I tell you!" insisted the voice of Harry Hazelton, as that young assistant engineer struggled with the crowd.

Then, on being recognized, Harry was allowed to reach the side of his chum.

"Mr. Reade!" called a husky-toned voice, "won't you order your men to let me through to see you? I want to talk with you about tonight's outrage."

Tom recognized the speaker as a man named Beasley, one of Paloma's most upright and courageous citizens.

"Let Mr. Beasley through," Tom called. "Don't block the streets, men. Remember, we've no right to do that."

A resounding cheer ascended at the sound of Tom's voice. In the light of the lanterns Tom was seen to be signaling with his hands for quiet, and the din soon died down.

"Mr. Reade," spoke Beasley, in a voice that shook with indignation, "the real men of this town would like an account of what has been going on here to-night. If Duff and his cronies have been up to anything that hurts the good name of the town we'd like the full particulars. You men there—don't let one of the rascals get away. Jim Duff and his gang will have to answer to the town of Paloma."

"Men," ordered Reade, "bring along the crew you caught in the cellar. Don't hurt them—remember how cowardly violence would be when we have everything in our own hands."

"The men of Paloma will do all the hurting," Mr. Beasley announced grimly.

Tom's own deliberate manner, and his manifest intention of not abusing his advantage impressed itself upon the decent men of Paloma, who now swarmed about the frightened captives from the cellar.

"I know 'em all," muttered Beasley. "I'll know 'em in the morning, too. So will you, friends!" he added, turning to the pressing crowds.

"Start Jim Duff on his travels now!" demanded one angry voice.

"By the Tree & Rope Short Line!" proposed another voice.

Jim was caught and held, despite his straggles. Active hands swarmed over his clothing, seeking for weapons.

"Gentlemen! Gentlemen!" appealed Tom sturdily, making his resonant voice travel far over the heads of the throng. "Will you honor me with your attention for three or four minutes?"

"Yep!" shouted back one voice.

"You bet!" came another voice.

"Go ahead and spout, Reade. We'll have the hanging, right after!"

There was nothing jovial in these responses. Tom Reade knew men well enough to recognize this fact. Moreover, Tom knew the plain, unvarnished, honest and deadly-in-earnest men of these south-western plains well enough to know the genuine fury of the crowd.

Arizona and New Mexico have long been held up as states where violence and lynch law prevail. The truth is that Arizona and New Mexico have no more lynchings than do many of the older states. An Arizona lynching can only follow an upheaval of public sentiment, when honest men are angered at having their fair fame sullied by the acts of blackguards.

"Friends," Tom went on, as soon as he could secure silence, "I am a newcomer among you. I have no right to tell you how to conduct your affairs, and I am not going to make that mistake. What you may do with Jim Duff, what you may do with others who damage the fair name of your town, is none of my business. For myself I want no revenge on these rascals. They have already been handled with much more roughness than they had time to show to me. I am satisfied to call the matter even."

"But we're not!" shouted an Arizona voice from the crowd.

"That's your own affair, gentlemen," Reade went on. "I wish to suggest—in fact, I beg of you—that you let these fellows go to-night. In the morning, when the sun is up, and after you have thought over the matter, you will be in a better position to give these fellows fair-minded justice—if you then still feel that something must be done to them. That is all I have to say, gentlemen. Now, Mr. Beasley, won't you follow with further remarks in this same line?"

Mr. Beasley looked more or less reluctant, but he presently complied with Reade's request. Then Tom called upon another prominent citizen of Paloma in the crowd for a speech.

"Let the coyotes go—until daylight," was the final verdict of the crowd, though there was an ominous note in the expressed decision.

In stony silence the crowd now parted to let Jim Duff and his fellows go away.

Within sixty seconds the last of them had run the gauntlet of contempt and vanished.

"Someone told me," scoffed Beasley, "that a gambler is a man of courage, polish, brains and good manners. I reckon Jim Duff isn't a real gambler, then."

"Yes, he is!" shouted another. "He's one of the real kind—sometimes smooth, but always bound to fatten on the money that belongs to other men."

"Jim can leave town, I reckon," grimly declared another old settler. "We have savings banks these days, and we don't need gamblers to carry our money for us."

"Speech, Reade! Speech!" insisted Mr. Beasley good-humoredly.

From some mysterious place a barrel was passed along from hand to hand. It was set down before the young chief engineer, and ready hands hoisted him to the upturned end of the barrel.

"Speech!" roared a thousand voices.

Tom, grinning good-humoredly, then waved his arms as though to still the tumult of voices. Gradually the cheering died down, then ceased.

Bang! sounded further down the Street, and the flash of a rifle was seen.

Tom Reade, his speech unmade, fell from the barrel into the arms of those crowded about him.

CHAPTER XV. MR. DANES INTRODUCES HIMSELF

Daylight found Jim Duff and some of his cronies of the night before either absent from Paloma, or else securely hidden.

Fred Ransom, the Colthwaite Company's representative, had also vanished.

Proprietor Ashby, of the Mansion House, was reported to be skulking in his hotel, as he did not show his face on the streets.

Morning also brought calmer counsel to the real men of Paloma. They were now glad that they had not sullied themselves by acts of violence.

No one, when daylight came, entertained the belief that Tom Reade would suffer from any further attempts at violence, for now the little coterie of so-called "bad men" in the town were thoroughly frightened.

Tom had not been hit by the rifle shot. He had fallen as a matter of precaution, fearing that a second shot would speed on the heels of the first.

The fellow who had fired that shot at Tom had not lingered long enough to place himself in risk of Arizona vengeance. Even before some of the men in the crowd had had time to discover that Reade, unhurt, was laughing over his escape, a score or more had darted down the street, only to find that the unknown whom they sought was safely out of the way.

"We'll search the town from one end to the other," one excited citizen had proposed.

"We'll make a night of it."

"Don't do anything of the sort," Tom had urged. "You'll terrorize hundreds of women and children, who have no knowledge of this affair. Jim Duff's little evening of celebration is ended and now the wisest thing for you to do is to return to your homes. Mr. Hawkins!"

"Here, sir," answered the superintendent of construction.

"Get our men together and return to camp. They'll need sleep against the toil of to-morrow. Let every man who wants to do so sleep an hour or two later in the morning. Men of the A., G. & N. M., accept my heartiest thanks for the splendid manner in which you turned out to help me, though as yet I'm ignorant of how it all came about."

Nor was it until the next day that Tom Reade learned from Hazelton just what had caused the laborers to tumble out of their beds and rush into town to serve him.

That night Tim Griggs had been prowling about the streets of Paloma, suspicious of Reade's enemies, and watching for the safety of the young chief engineer who had saved him from the savage appetite of the Man-killer quicksand.

It had chanced that Tim had caught a glimpse of the finish of the fight on the street, and was just in time to see the young chief engineer lifted and carried into that unoccupied house, the property of the hotel man, Ashby.

Tim's first instinct had been to seek help in town—in that very neighborhood. Tim was suspicious, and afraid that he might by mistake appeal to some of Tom's enemies.

So, while running through the streets searching for Hazelton, Tim had espied an automobile standing idle in front of a house. Having some acquaintance with automobiles, Tim had cranked up and leaped into the vehicle, speeding straight to camp, where he gave the alarm. Men answered by hundreds, Mendoza keeping his Mexicans in camp to watch the property there.

Harry was aroused by the tumult, for he had just gone to his room, intending to turn in.

Having roused the camp, Tim ran the car back to town at the head of the swarming little army and returned to the spot where he had seized the automobile.

"It's all over now, old fellow," Tom declared to his chum cheerily, rising from his office chair as one of the whistles blew and the men knocked off for their noonday meal. "What happened last night won't happen again."

"Just the same, Tom, I almost wish you'd carry a pistol after this," Harry remarked, as the two engineers went to their horses, mounted and started toward town for their own meal.

"Bosh!" almost snapped Tom. "You know my opinion of pistols. They are for policemen, soldiers and others who have real need to go armed. Only a coward would pack a pistol day by day without needing it."

So the matter was dropped for the time being.

At the hotel Tom and Harry went to their accustomed seats in the dining room. Their food was brought and the two young engineers fell to work cheerfully. Just then a well-dressed man of perhaps thirty years entered the dining, room, spoke to one of the waiters, and came over to the engineers' table.

"Messrs. Reade and Hazelton?" he inquired pleasantly.

"Yes," Harry nodded.

"May I make myself known?" asked the stranger. "My name is Danes—Frank Danes."

Harry in turn gave his own name and that of Tom.

"I wonder if you would think it intruding if I invited myself to join you at this table?" the stranger went on.

"By no means," Tom responded cordially. "We'll be glad of your company. It will stop Hazelton and myself from talking too much shop."

"Oh, by all means talk shop," begged Danes, as he slipped into a chair at one side of the table. "I shall enjoy it, for I am interested in you both. In fact, I took the liberty of asking the waiter to point you gentlemen out to me."

"So?" Tom inquired.

Danes had the appearance of being a well-to-do easterner, and announced himself as a resident of Baltimore.

For some minutes the three chatted pleasantly, Harry, however, doing most of the talking for the engineers. When Tom spoke it was generally to put some question.

"Do you ever permit visitors to go out to the Man-killer?" Danes inquired toward the end of the meal.

"Sometimes," Tom answered.

"I shall be very grateful if you will accord me that privilege."

"We shall be very glad to invite you out there some time," Tom answered pleasantly.

"To-day?" pressed the stranger. "I have nothing to do this afternoon."

"Some other day would suit better, if you can arrange it conveniently," Reade suggested, as he rose.

Then they left Danes, securing their horses and riding back over the scorching desert.

"How do you like Danes?" Harry asked, after they had ridden some distance. "He seems a very pleasant fellow."

"Very pleasant," Tom nodded.

"Why didn't you let him come along?"

"Because I don't like Danes' employers."

"His employers?" Harry repeated, puzzled.

"Yes; he is employed by the Colthwaite Company."

"What?" Hazelton started in astonishment. "How do you know that, Tom?"

"I don't know it, but I'm sure of it, just the same," was Reade's answer.

"It maybe so," Harry agreed. "What makes you suspect him?"

"Well, in the first place, Danes, if that's his name—said he hailed from Baltimore. Yet he had none of that soft, delightful southern accent that you and I have noticed in the voices of real southern men. Danes uses two or three words, at times, that are distinctly Chicago slang. Moreover, I'm certain that the man knows a good deal about engineering work, though he won't admit it."

"We'll have to watch him, then," muttered Harry.

"We don't need to tell him anything, nor do we need to bring him out here to see how we are filling in the Man-killer. If we don't tell Danes much he may not last long. The Colthwaite people ought soon to grow tired of keeping agents here who don't succeed in hindering our work."

"Whew! I shall be glad of a sleep to-night, after all the excitement of last night," declared Hazelton, as the young engineers rode into Paloma at the close of the day's work.

On the porch, lolling in a reclining chair with his feet elevated to the railing, sat Frank Danes.

"Back from toil, gentlemen?" was his pleasant greeting.

"Long enough to get sufficient sleep to carry us through to-morrow," was Tom Reade's unruffled response.

"You do look tired," assented Danes, rising and coming toward them. "Yet I hear that, personally, you don't have hard work to do."

"We don't work at all, if you take that view of it," Harry retorted. "Yet there's a thing called responsibility, and many wise men have declared that it takes more out of a man than hours of toiling with pick and shovel."

"Oh, I can believe that's so," agreed Danes. "Going into dinner now?"

"After a bath and a change of clothing," Tom replied.

"Then, if you really don't mind, I'll wait and dine at the same table with you."

"If you can wait that long we shall be charmed to have your company," Tom assured him as the young engineers stepped inside.

Frank Danes half started as they left him.

"Reade's tone sounded a bit peculiar," muttered the newcomer to himself. "I wonder why? Perhaps I have forced myself a little too much upon him and Reade has taken a dislike to me."

If Tom had taken a dislike to the newcomer, Danes could not be sure of it from the young chief engineer's manner at table. Harry Hazelton, too, was almost gracious during the meal.

"They're a pair of half-smart, half-simple boobs," decided Danes, as he smoked a cigar alone after dinner.

"Tom, I think your great intellect has gone astray for once," remarked Hazelton, in the privacy of their room upstairs.

"I never knew that I had any great intellect," Reade laughed. "However, I was born to be suspicious once in a while. I suppose you were referring to Frank Danes."

"Yes; and he appears to be a mighty decent fellow."

"I'm sure I hope he is," yawned Tom. "I'm willing to give him the benefit of the doubt. I'm going to bed, Harry. What do you say?"

Hazelton was agreeable. Within twenty minutes both young engineers were sound asleep.

It was after midnight when cries of "fire!" from the street aroused them.

Tom Reade threw open the door to be greeted by a cloud of stifling smoke.

"Hustle, Harry!" he gasped, making a rush to get into his clothing. "We can get out, I think, but we haven't any time to spare. This old trap is ablaze. It won't last many minutes!"

Trained in the alarms and the hurries of camp life, the young engineers all but sprang into their clothes.

"Come on, Harry!" urged Tom, throwing open the door. "We can make it."

They started, when, from the floor above, a woman's frantic appeals for help reached them. Children's cries were added to hers.

"Get to the street, Harry!" shouted Tom. "I'm going upstairs. There'd be no satisfaction for me in reaching the street if I abandoned that woman and her babies to their fate. One of us can do the job as well as two!"

CHAPTER XVI. DANES SHIVERS ON A HOT NIGHT

Almost immediately after the cries of "fire" the bell at the fire station pealed out.

Paloma's volunteer fire department turned out quickly, running to the scene with a hand engine, two hose reels and a ladder truck.

By this time, however, the whole of Paloma appeared to be lighted up with the brisk blaze. Tongues of flame shot skyward from the burning hotel, while small blazing embers dropped freely into the street.

"Is everyone out? Everyone safe? Anyone missing?" panted Carter, the young proprietor of the Cactus House.

The disturbed guests ranged themselves about Carter, who looked them over swiftly.

"Where are Mrs. Gerry and her two babies?" demanded the hotel man, his cheeks blanching.

None answered, for no one had seen the woman and her children.

"They must be in the house," cried Carter.

At that instant a woman's face appeared, briefly, at a window on the third floor. Her piercing cry rang out, then her face vanished, a cloud of smoke driving her from the open window.

"Hustle the ladders along!" begged the hotel man hoarsely. "We must rescue that woman and her children. Her husband will be here in morning. What can we say to him if we allow his wife and children to perish in the flames?"

In a few moments a long ladder had been hauled off the track and brave men rushed it to the wall, two men starting to ascend the moment it was in place.

In another moment they came sliding down, balked. Flames had enveloped the upper end of the ladder. It had to be hauled down, buckets of water being dashed over the blazing sides.

"You can't get a ladder up on any part of that wall to the third floor," called the chief of the fire department hoarsely, as he broke through a thick veil of smoke. "You'll have to try the rear."

"Where are Reade and Hazelton?" called a voice.

"Reade!"

"Hazelton!"

There was no answer. A hundred men turned, looking blankly at their nearest fellows.

"They've gone down in the flames!" called another voice.

"Reade and Hazelton have lost their lives!"

"That'll make their enemies happy!" groaned one man, and other voices took it up.

"Carter," shouted one big man, running to the proprietor, "if this blaze is the work of a fire-bug, then look for Reade and Hazelton's enemies. They have the most to gain by the death of those young fellows!"

A hoarse yell went up from the crowd. All of a sudden it seemed plain to every man present that the hatred for Tom and Harry in certain quarters fully accounted for the fire.

"Get a rope! Lynch somebody!" shouted one voice after another.

"First of all, let's find a way to get that woman and her babies out!" Carter appealed, frantically.

Scores of voices took up this cry, and numbers of men hastened around to the rear of the little hotel in the wake of the laddermen.

"We must find Reade and Hazelton, too," shouted others.

"Then we'll lynch someone for this night's business!"

The cry was taken up hoarsely.

Two ladders were quickly hoisted at the rear. Almost before they had begun to hoist, the laddermen and spectators felt that it was a useless attempt.

Nor did the doors and passages seem to offer any better avenue of escape.

Chug, chug, chug! sounded a touring car close at hand. An automobile stopped, Dr. Furniss jumping out.

"Anyone in danger!" shouted the young doctor.

"Yes; a woman and her children. Also Reade and Hazelton!"

"It's all right, then," nodded Furniss, looking relieved. "Tom Reade and Harry Hazelton have gone to the aid of the woman."

"If I could only believe that!" gasped Proprietor Carter. "We've tried the ladders, and we've tried the corridors of the house. It's a raging furnace in there."

Dr. Furniss looked on rather calmly.

"I'm merely wondering on which side of the house those two engineers will appear with the woman and her children," he declared.

For the fourth time a ladder was being vainly raised at the rear. Suddenly a shout rang out. In the basement a window was unexpectedly knocked out from the inside.

Through the way thus cleared leaped a young man so blackened with smoke as to be unrecognizable, though it was Hazelton.

Before those who first espied the young man recovered from their surprise, a pair of arms from the inside handed out the body of a child to Hazelton.

Then came another child. Next the senseless body of a woman was handed out.

Dr. Furniss was the first to recover, from delighted amazement. In a bound he was on the spot, taking care of one of the children himself and bawling to others to bring the rest of the family.

Tom Reade, looking more like a burnt-cork minstrel in hard luck than like his usual self, sprang through the window way and followed.

"Here, you people—stand back!" roared Tom, elbowing his way along. "Dr. Furniss and his patients want room and air. Stand back!"

"It's Reade!" yelled a dozen men in delight.

"Well, what of it?" asked Tom coolly, as he followed Furniss. "Was there anyone here who expected that I'd be lost?"

"Hurrah! Where's Hazelton?"

"Who wants me?" demanded the other unrecognizable, smoke-blackened figure.

"They're both safe!"

"Oh—cut it out," begged Tom good-humoredly. "You can't lose an engineer or even kill him. Doc, what's the report?"

"All three are alive," replied Dr. Furniss, "but they'll need care and nursing. Here, help me place them in my car. Someone get in and ride with me—I'll need help. You, Reade!"

"No," responded Tom with emphasis, as he looked down at his discolored self. "If the lady saw me when she opened her eyes, she'd faint again. I'd scare the kiddies into convulsions. A bath for me!"

A man from the crowd quickly stepped into the tonneau of the car, ready to care for the woman and her children while the physician drove his car home.

"Hello, Reade! My congratulations on your getting out. 'Twas a brave deed, too, to save that poor woman and her children."

Frank Danes pressed through the crowd about the car, reaching out to seize Reade's hand.

Into Tom's face flashed a sudden look that few had ever seen there.

It was a look full of contempt that the young chief engineer bent on the man who had greeted him.

"Your hand!" cried Danes, in a voice ringing with admiration.

"Don't you touch me!" warned Reade, his voice vibrating with anger.

"Why—what—" began Danes, then reached his own right hand for Tom's.

"Make way for this 'gentleman' to fall!" roared Reade, then swung a crushing blow that landed squarely in Danes's face.

The latter went down in a heap.

There had been no explanation of the seemingly unprovoked blow, but the crowd surged forward, snatching Danes's body up as though he were something of which these men were anxious to be rid.

"Did he set the hotel afire?" demanded one man in husky tones.

"Did he?" chorused the crowd.

"Lemme through! Here's a rope!"

Then followed wild sounds that could not be distinguished as words. These men of Paloma seemed bent upon fighting for the possession of Frank Danes, who, having now recovered his senses, emitted shrill appeals for mercy.

"Here's the fire-bug! Here's the human match!"

"To the nearest tree!"

"I've got the rope ready!"

In another thirty seconds Frank Danes would have been dangling from a limb of the nearest tree. Again Reade and Hazelton sprang into action.

"Stand back, men—please do!" begged Tom, fighting his way through the thinnest side of the crowd. "Don't kill any man without a trial."

"You know that this tenderfoot fired the hotel, don't you?" asked one man hoarsely.

"I've reason to suspect that he did—"

"That's enough for us!" roared a hundred voices.

"But I've no positive proof of Danes' guilt," Tom insisted.

"To the tree with him!"

"Not while I've breath left in my body!" Tom blazed forth desperately. "Come, Harry!"

Hazelton sprang to his chum's side, the two fighting desperately to drive away the men who held Frank Danes captive.

"Wait a few hours at least, men!" Tom appealed earnestly. "Don't do anything now that you'll be sorry for to-morrow."

Other men of calm judgment began to see the force of Reade's remarks.

Tom and Harry were swiftly backed by such reinforcements that the trembling wretch was torn from his would-be destroyers.

"Reade," sobbed Frank Danes, "as long as I live I'll never forget your splendid conduct."

"Shut up!" retorted Tom roughly. "I don't want to have to knock you down again. It might start a riot that no man could quell."

"Pass the skulking tenderfoot out to us!" implored some of the men on the edge of the crowd, among whom was the man with the spare rope.

"No! We won't disgrace the town with a lynching," Tom shot back. "Wait until cool judgment has had time to do its work."

"Bear a hand there!" roared Harry. "Help the firemen to save the next building. Follow me!"

Thus led, the fickle crowd started to the aid of the firemen.

"Come with me, Danes," whispered Tom hoarsely, sternly. "Keep your distance, however, or I shall lay violent hands on you."

Once out of the glare of light cast by the burning of the hotel, Tom Reade pointed down a dark side street.

"There's your way, Danes," whispered Reade. "Skip! Be far from Paloma by daylight—or nothing will save you."

"Do you consider me responsible for that fire?" faltered Danes.

"Hazelton and I went through that fire," Tom retorted sternly. "We had a hard fight to save that woman and her babies, and were nearly choked with the fumes of the coal oil with which the fire was kindled. I couldn't swear, in court, Danes, that you started the blaze, but your coat and your hands have the odor of coal oil."

Dane's face turned pale, his legs shaking under him.

"So, you see," continued Tom savagely, "you'll do well to escape before anyone else notices the smell of coal oil on you."

"You've been mighty good to me—and I—" chattered Danes.

"Shut up, as I advised you before!" rasped Tom Reade. "I've been as good to you as I'd be to a rattlesnake. Get out of Arizona before the men of this town suspect—understand—you?"

"I will," Frank Danes agreed, his teeth chattering.

"Don't ever show your face again in this part of the world."

"I won't, Reade. Again, my thanks—"

"Shut up!" Tom insisted. "Thanks from you would make me feel like a traitor to the community. Skip! Carry word to the Colthwaite Company, however, that their latest scheme against us has failed like the others!"

At mention of the Colthwaits, Danes turned and fled in earnest.

"That was their second attempt," muttered Tom grimly, as he turned back to where the flames still held dominion. "I wonder if I shall be as lucky when the third attempt against me is made?"

CHAPTER XVII. TIM GRIGGS "GETS HIS"

In another hour the spot where the hotel had stood was marked only by a shapeless mass of smoking embers.

The citizens of the town went back to their beds. Mrs. Gerry and her children had recovered consciousness and had found a friendly lodging for the night.

The rescue performed by Tom and Harry had been a simple enough achievement.

Shut off from every other means of escape, they remembered the dumbwaiter that ran from the kitchen up to the floors above.

The two little children were sent down on the dumb-waiter, Harry riding on the top of the wooden frame. Mrs. Gerry's rescue was delayed until Harry could send the dumb-waiter up to the third floor, where she and Tom awaited its return. Aided by Tom, she descended to the kitchen without accident; then Tom followed, sliding down the rope. It was but the work of a moment to break through the basement window and pass the woman and her children out to safety.

Morning found Proprietor Carter somewhat resigned to his loss. True, the hotel had been destroyed and the embers must be removed, but both building and contents had been fairly well insured.

"I'm a few thousand out," said the hotel man philosophically, "but I have my ground yet, and, the insurance money will allow me to rebuild., and put up a more modern hotel. Of course I'll be a few thousand dollars in debt, to start with, but after a short while I'll have earned the money that I've lost."

"Why did you smile when poor Carter was talking about his loss?" demanded Harry, as the chums strolled away in search of breakfast.

"Did I?" asked Tom, looking suddenly very, sober.

"There was a broad grin on your face?"

"Carter didn't see it, did he?"

"I don't know; but why, the grin, Tom?"

"I'll tell you after I see what answer I receive to a telegram that I've sent."

"Tom Reade, you always were provoking!"

"Now I'm doubly so, eh?"

"Oh, well, I don't care," muttered Harry. "I can wait; I'm not very nosey."

By noon General Manager Ellsworth arrived on the scene of the labors of the young engineers, out at the site of the big quicksand.

"You can run the work here this afternoon, Harry," Tom declared. "I shall want to put in my time with Mr. Ellsworth."

"Was he the answer to your telegram?"

Tom offered no further information, but hurried away to meet the general manager, who had come out to camp in an automobile hired at Paloma. Manager and chief engineer now toured slowly toward town, Harry watching them as long as they were in sight.

"Tom has something big in the wind," muttered Hazelton. "It must be something about the hotel fire. What can it be? At any rate, I'll wager it's something that pleases my chum wonderfully."

Nor did Tom return until late in the afternoon. He came back alone.

"Well?" demanded Harry.

"Yes," nodded Tom. "It's well."

"What is?"

"The game."

"What is the game?"

"When you hear about it—" Reade began.

"Yes, yes—"

"Then you'll know."

"Tom Reade, do you know, I believe I'm quite ready and willing to thrash you?" cried Harry in exasperation.

"Please don't," Tom begged.

"Then tell me what you've been so mightily mysterious about."

"I will," returned Reade. "I'd have told you hours ago, Harry, only I'm afraid you would have been demoralized with disappointment if the thing had failed to go through. Harry, to-day I've been meddling in other people's business. Congratulate me! I put it through without getting myself thumped or even disliked, by anyone. Both sides to the deal are 'tickled to death,' as the saying runs."

"You said you were going to tell me," remarked Hazelton, trying hard to restrain his curiosity for a minute or two longer.

"Sit down and listen," Tom urged his chum, handing him a chair in their little shack of an office.

Then, indeed, Tom did pour forth the whole story. As Harry listened a broad grin of contentment appeared on his face, for one of Hazelton's lovable weaknesses was his desire to see other people get ahead.

Just as Tom finished, a figure darkened the doorway.

"I'm ready to go, sir," announced Tim Griggs.

"Go where?" inquired Harry.

"I've fired Griggs," observed Tom Reade.

"What! After all that he did for you the other night?" demanded Hazelton, aghast. "After the man saved your—"

"Oh, I'm quite satisfied to be fired, Mr. Hazelton," Tim Griggs broke in. "In fact, I'm very grateful to Mr. Reade. He has certainly given me a big boost forward in the world."

"What are you going to do now, Griggs?" Harry asked.

"You'd better address him as 'Mr. Griggs,' Harry," Tom hinted. "He is a foreman now, at six dollars a day, and entitled to his Mister."

"Foreman?" Harry repeated, while Gregg's grin broadened.

"Yes," Tom continued. "Mr. Griggs is to be foreman on the new job that I've just been telling you about in town. After this, if Mr. Griggs is careful to behave himself, he's likely always to be a foreman on some job or other for the A., G. & N. M."

Harry sprang forward, seizing the hand of Tim Griggs and shaking it with enthusiasm.

"Bully old Griggs! Lucky old Griggs!" Hazelton bubbled forth. "Mr. Griggs, you'll believe from now on what I've always believed—that it's a great piece of luck in itself to be one of Tom Reade's friends."

"It surely has been great luck for me, sir," Griggs answered. "The best part of all," he added, with a husky note in his voice, "is what it means to that little girl of mine. When I get into town to-night I in going to sit down and write that little daughter a long letter all about the grand news. She'll be proud of her dad's good luck! She's only eight years old, but she's a great little reader, and she writes me letters longer than my own."

"If you'll wait a minute, Mr. Griggs," proposed Tom, "we'll be able to give you a ride into town. The general manager gave me authority to rent and use an automobile after this. It's out there waiting now."

The new foreman gratefully accepted the invitation. Within five minutes the chauffeur had stopped the car in Paloma and Tim Griggs got out to go to his new boarding place in the town.

"God bless you, Mr. Reade!" he said huskily, holding out his band. "You've done a lot for me—and my little girl!"

"No more than you've done for me," smiled Tom. "Anyway, you haven't received more than you deserve, and you never will in this little old world of ours."

"I don't know about that," replied the new foreman, a sudden flush rising to his weather-beaten face. "It all seems too good to be true."

"You'll find it to be true enough when you draw your next pay, Griggs," laughed Tom. "Then you'll realize that you aren't dreaming. In the meantime your dinner is getting cold at your boarding place. Don't let your new job spoil your appetite."

When Tom and Harry rode into town at noon the following day they beheld a scene of great activity at the site of the destroyed Cactus House. All the blackened debris had been carted away during the morning by a large force of men. Now, derricks lay in place, to be erected in the afternoon. A steam shovel had been all but installed and a large stationary engine rested on nearly completed foundations.

George Ashby, proprietor of the Mansion House, who had dared, during the last two days, to show himself a little more openly on the streets of Paloma, halted just as Tom and Harry stepped out of the automobile to look over the scene of Foreman Griggs's morning labors.

"Looks as if the Cactus House might be rebuilt," remarked Ashby, burning with curiosity.

"No," said Tom briefly.

"Carter is going to change the name?" inquired Ashby.

"No. Carter doesn't own this land any more."

"He doesn't own the land?" Ashby asked. "What's going to be put up here, then? A business block?"

For a moment Ashby thrilled with joy. Of late the Cactus House had seriously cut in on the profits of the Mansion House. Ashby had, in fact, been running behind. Now, if the Mansion House were to be henceforth the only hotel in town, Ashby saw a chance to prosper on a more than comfortable scale.

"Ashby," Tom went on, rather frigidly, "I won't waste many words, for I'm afraid I don't like you well enough to talk very much to you. The A., G. & N. M. has bought this land from Mr. Carter. The railroad is going to erect here one of the finest hotels in this part of Arizona. It will have every modern convenience, and will make your hotel look like a mill boarding house by contrast. When the new hotel is completed it will be leased to Mr. Carter. With his insurance money, and the price of the land in bank, Carter will have capital for embarking in the hotel business on a scale that will make this end of Arizona sit up and do some hard looking."

As he listened Proprietor Ashby's jaw dropped. His color came and went. He swallowed hard, while his hands worked convulsively. With the fine new hotel that was coming to Paloma the owner of the Mansion House saw himself driven hopelessly into the background. "Reade, this new hotel game is some of your doings," growled the hotel man.

"I'm proud to say that it is partly my doing," Tom admitted, with a smile. "Harry, let's go along to the restaurant. I'm hungry."

As the two young engineers stepped into the car and were driven away, Ashby dug his fingernails into the palms of his hands.

"So I'm to be beaten out of the hotel game here, am I!" the hotel man asked himself, gritting his teeth. "I'm to be driven out by Reade, the fellow whom I once kicked out of my hotel! Oh—well, all right!"

CHAPTER XVIII. TRAGEDY CAPS THE TEST

"Pass the signal!" directed Tom.

A railroad man with a flag made several swift moves. Down the track an engineman, in his cab, answered with a short blast of, the whistle. Then he threw over the lever, and a train of ten flat cars started along in the engine's wake.

It was the first test—the "small test," Tom called it—of the track that now extended across the surface of the Man-killer.

On each flat car were piled ten tons of steel rails, to be used further along in the construction work. With engine, cars and all, the load amounted to one hundred and fifty tons, the pressure of which would be exerted over a comparatively short strip of the new track that now glistened over the Man-killer.

Mounted on his pony, Harry Hazelton had galloped a considerable distance down the track. Now, halted, he had turned his pony's head about, watching eagerly the on-coming train.

For two weeks the laborers had been working on the roadbed now running over the Man-killer. Ties had been laid and rails fastened down. Apparently the Man-killer had done its worst and had been balked, a seemingly secure roadbed now resting on the once treacherous quicksand.

Construction trains, short and lightly laden, had been moving out over the newly filled in soil for many days, but the train now starting at the edge of the terrible Man-killer was heavier than any equipment that had before been run over the ground.

The president of the A., G. & N. M. R. R. was there, flanked by half a dozen of the leading directors of the road. There were other officials there, including General Manager Ellsworth.

"I see Hazelton out yonder," murmured the president of the road. "But where's that young man Reade, now at the moment when the success of his work is being tested?"

"Goodness knows," rejoined Mr. Ellsworth. "As likely as not he's back in the office, taking a nap after having given the engineman his signal."

"Asleep!" repeated the president. "Can he be so indolent or so indifferent as that?"

"You may always depend upon Tom Reade to do something that wouldn't be expected of him," laughed Mr. Ellsworth. "It isn't that he slights big duties, or even pretends to do. If he has vanished, and has gone to sleep, then it is because he feels so sure of his work that he takes no further interest in the test that is being made."

"But if an accident should happen?" asked the president of the A. G. & N. M. R. R.

"Then I can promise you that you'd see Reade, on his pony, shooting ahead as fast as he could go to the scene of the trouble."

These more important railroad officials had come out to camp in automobiles. Now they followed on foot as the train rolled on to the land reclaimed from the Man-killer.

Superintendent Hawkins and his foremen also went along on foot to observe whether the track sank ever so little at any point.

It was none of Harry Hazelton's particular business to watch whether the tracks sank slightly. That duty could be better performed by the foremen who had had charge of the track laying. Yet Hazelton, as he watched, found himself growing impatient.

"Here!" Harry called to a near-by laborer. "Take my horse, please."

In another instant the young assistant engineer was on foot, following the slowly moving train as it rolled along over the ground where, months before, not even a man could have strolled with safety.

"Do you see any sagging of the track, Mr. Rivers?" Harry called.

"No, sir. Not as much as a sixteenth of an inch at any point," responded the foreman. "The job has been a big success."

"We can tell that better after the track has held loads of from five to eight hundred tons," Harry rejoined. "I believe, however, that we have the tricks of the savage old Man-killer nailed."

Exultation throbbed in Harry's heart. Outwardly, he did not trust himself to reveal his great delight. He still followed, watching anxiously, until the train had passed safely over the Man-killer.

Then a great cheer went up from more than a thousand throats, for many people had come out from Paloma to watch the test.

The train had gone a quarter of a mile past the western edge of the huge and once treacherous quicksand. Now the engine was on a temporary turn-table, waiting to be turned and switched back to bring the train back over the Man-killer at a swift gait.

"Where's Mr. Reade?" called the president of the road, gazing backward. "Someone go for him. I wish him to be here to see the test made with the train under fast speed."

"I'll get Reade, sir," answered Harry, motioning to have his pony brought to him.

Hazelton vanished in a cloud of desert dust.

When he next appeared there was another pony, and Reade astride it.

"You sent for me, sir," said Tom, riding close to the president, then dismounting.

"Yes," Mr. Reade. "I believed that you should be here to see the test train return."

"Very good, sir," was Tom's quiet reply. He signaled for a workman to come and take charge of his pony.

In a few minutes the short but heavy train started, gaining headway rapidly. By the time it struck the edge of the possibly conquered quicksand it was moving at the rate of forty miles an hour.

Across the Man-killer the train continued for a mile in the direction of Paloma.

"Now, let us all inspect the track," suggested the president of the railroad company. "Call up the autos."

"Will you let me make a suggestion, sir!" queried Tom.

"Go ahead, Mr. Reade."

"Then, sir, let Mr. Hazelton and myself ride out along the track first, that we may see if the whole course is safe."

"That heavy train just went over at fast speed and nothing disastrous happened," protested the president.

"Probably the entire course is still safe, sir?" Tom assented. "Yet, on the other hand, it is possible that the fast moving train may have started the quicksand at some point. The next object that passes over, even if no heavier than an automobile, may meet with disaster. Mr. Hazelton and I can soon satisfy ourselves as to whether the roadbed has sagged at any point along the way. We shall ride nothing heavier than mustangs."

"There is something in what you say, Mr. Reade. Go ahead. We will wait until we have your report."

Tom and Harry accordingly mounted, riding off at a trot. Yet at some sections of the line they rode so slowly, studying the ground attentively, that it was fully half an hour before they had crossed the further edge of the Man-killer.

"The engineers are signaling us, Mr. President," reported General Manager Ellsworth. "They are motioning us to go forward."

Accordingly the party of railway officials entered their automobiles and started slowly off over the Man-killer.

"Ride back and meet them, Harry," Tom suggested. "Show them that one point that we noticed."

Hazelton accordingly dug his heels into the flank of his pony, starting off at a gallop.

Two or three minutes passed. Then Mr. Ellsworth leaped from his seat in the foremost automobile, standing erect in the car and pointing excitedly.

"Look there!" he shouted lustily. "What's happening?"

Away off, at the further side of the Man-killer, a horseman had suddenly ridden into sight from behind a sand pile. His swiftly moving pony had gotten within three hundred yards of the chief engineer before Tom looked up to behold the newcomer.

From where the railroad officials watched they could hear nothing, though they saw a succession of indistinct spittings from something in the right hand of the horseman.

"It's a revolver the fellow's shooting at Mr. Reade!" gasped Superintendent Hawkins, leaping into the car beside the general manager. "Turn your speed on, man—make a lightning lash across the Man-killer!"

Away shot the automobile, not wholly to the liking of two eastern men who sat in the directors' car.

Tom Reade had realized his danger. Having nothing with which to fight, Reade had sprung his horse eastward and was racing for life.

The unknown had emptied his weapon, but that did not deter him, for, continuing his wild pursuit, the stranger could be seen to draw another automatic revolver.

The bullets striking all about Tom's pony ploughed up the sand.

Within a minute the men in the speeding automobile were close enough to hear the sputtering crackle of the pistol shots.

"There goes Hazelton right into the face of death!" gasped Mr. Ellsworth, who remained in a standing position. "Foolish of the boy, but magnificent!"

Harry had turned some time before, but now those in the automobile saw that Hazelton was riding squarely to Tom's side, despite the constant fusillade of bullets.

Both pistols were now emptied, but the pursuer, letting his reins fall on the neck of his madly galloping pony, was inserting fresh cartridges in the magazine chambers of his pistols.

CHAPTER XIX. THE SECRET OF ASHBY'S CUNNING

At a considerable distance behind the automobile came another rescue party. This was made up of about two score of Arizona horsemen. Many of these men were armed. At the saddle bows of some of the hung raw-hide lariats that the owners unwound as they sped forward.

Tom Reade, with the pursuer slowly, but steadily gaining upon him, had discovered the identity of the man who seemed bent on his destruction.

As Hazelton drew nearer Tom waved his left hand frantically at his chum.

"Turn about, Harry! Ride back like the wind!" shouted Tom. "It's Ashby, and he's shooting to kill. About face—you young idiot!"

Harry took no notice of the warning, reining in only slightly, then wheeling and riding in a line with Reade, though about forty feet to one side of him.

Ashby, a wild light in his eyes, heavily armed, and riding madly, kept up a continuous fire in his effort to destroy the young chief engineer.

Honk! Honk! honk! came the warning from the automobile horn. The car dashed at full speed toward the vengeful rider, as though about to run him down.

George Ashby, however, was not easily intimidated. One swift glance had assured him that the automobile bore no armed men. He therefore merely swung his horse out of the path of the on-coming car and continued to aim at Reade, though he now took more time between shots. On Hazelton he did not waste a shot.

Helplessly and vainly the automobile whizzed by pursuer and pursued.

"Ashby, stop this madness!" cried Mr. Ellsworth hoarsely.

The pursuing rider never faltered. Now the party of Arizona horsemen were riding nearer. Two or three of the leaders drew revolvers, opening fire on the mad hotel man, though the range was as yet too great for effective work.

In another thirty seconds George Ashby would doubtless have dropped to the dust of the dessert, riddled with lead. Suddenly, however, he gave his horse's head a sharp turn to the right. In an instant he was riding back, shooting no more, and Tom Reade had passed safely out of range.

With wild whoops the Paloma horsemen dashed on. Their mounts were not spent as was that of the hotel man.

"Don't shoot the fellow, if you can help it!" Tom Reade had called, as the horsemen swept by him. "Rope Ashby if you can."

Suddenly the hotel man's mount was seen to stagger slightly. It was sufficient to pitch Ashby, who was not on his guard.

With wilder whoops the Arizona men spurred their ponies on. There was a whirring of lariats and no less than three nooses had fallen over the hotel man's head.

There came a brief interval in which the men, swooping down on the captive, concealed him from the view of others.

Out of this crush soon came order. Then it was seen that Ashby had been roped securely and was being led back to the railroad camp.

"We've got the scoundrel, with four ropes hitched to him," called one of the captors.

"One rope will be enough as soon as we can find a tree."

The party was riding into the railroad camp now, and a dense crowd pressed forward to see the face of the keeper of the Mansion House.

Ashby was chuckling gleefully. If any fear of the consequences of his lawless behavior oppressed him, he was far from betraying the fact.

"Be gentle with him, friends," Tom urged, riding forward.

"Yes; we ought to be gentle with every rattlesnake," came an answer from the crowd.

Ashby laughed harshly.

"You can't hurt me, neighbors," declared the hotel man. "I'm bullet proof. Any man who fires at me will find that the bullet will rebound and bit him. Tie me up to a tree, if you like. You'll find that I won't choke. I'll just slide back to earth as often as you tie me up."

"Just what I thought," murmured Tom.

"What do you think?" demanded Mr. Ellsworth from the car.

"The man's as mad as a March hare," replied Reade.

"Humph! He's merely shamming," retorted the general manager.

"Stow the funny business, Ashby!" came the advice from the crowd. "You can't fool us into believing that you're crazy."

"Crazy?" repeated the hotel man, a look of amazement creeping into his face. "Of course I'm not crazy. I'm the only sane man in this crowd."

Men began to look wonderingly at the hotel man, though many still believed that Ashby was cleverly shamming insanity in order to save his neck from being stretched.

"Doe Furniss! Come over here!" called Reade. "Gentlemen, this is a question for Doe Furniss. Don't think of doing anything to the fellow until you've heard from Doc. Make way for the doctor, gentlemen."

At a sign from Dr. Furniss the captors led Ashby's horse onward until the office shack was reached. Here two men freed the captive from his horse and led him inside. Dr. Furniss followed them and the door was closed.

"Let's get away from here," urged Tom Reade. "A big crowd hanging about is sure to excite the poor fellow."

"Reade, you're too soft and easy," grunted a Paloma man in the crowd. "The only thing that makes Ashby crazy is that he didn't get you."

"He did 'get' me, however," laughed Tom, displaying four bullet holes through his shirtsleeves, and two more that pierced his hat. "Ashby got as much of me as I'd want any marksman to get."

Having withdrawn to a distance, the crowd waited.

It was nearly half an hour before Dr. Furniss stepped outside. Now he walked swiftly over to the edge of the crowd.

"Gentlemen," remarked the physician, "you are justified in feeling very well pleased that you didn't lynch Ashby. The poor fellow is as insane as a man could well be. He imagines Mr. Reade has hurt his business and is determined to kill him. I'll send for a straightjacket and then we'll hustle him away to the asylum."

At this moment a wild yell sounded from the shack, to be echoed from the crowd. George Ashby, seemingly possessed of the strength of half a dozen men, had wrenched himself free of his captors, felling both like a flash. Then the hotel man leaped to his horse, freeing it and starting off at a mad gallop.

Instantly a score of men set off after the fugitive, swinging their lariats as they rode.

Crack! Crack! Bang!

Snatching still another automatic revolver from one of his saddle bags, Ashby was now firing at those riding behind him.

The line of horsemen wavered somewhat. They might have fired in return, and have brought down their quarry, but no brave man likes to think of shooting a lunatic.

So, still firing as he went, Ashby once more reached the edge of the quicksand.

Now, riding as fast as he could urge his pony, the hotel man dashed out on the Man-killer.

Nor was he riding over the part that had been rendered safe by the young engineers.

Instead, he was riding to the southward of the railroad property—straight out where he was likely to find a speedy death in the engulfing sands.

"Stop, Ashby! Come back!" shouted a dozen voices. "You'll be swallowed up in the quick-sands."

Brave as they were, the pursuers now rein up sharply. It seemed to them sheer madness to ride out thus to their certain deaths.

"Ashby is crazy, all right," remarked bronzed man. "None but an insane man would ride out there."

Somewhat tardily automobile parties started in pursuit. These vehicles were halted at the edge of the quicksand. Tom and Harry had also come this far.

In the background the halted crowd watched in suspense as George Ashby galloped over the treacherous sand.

Several times the pony's hoofs were seen to sink, yet each time the animal seemed able to draw his feet out of the sand and go on again.

"It's a crazy man's luck," cried an Arizona man thickly. "Of course, here and there on the Man-killer there are safe, sound spots, and Ashby is having the luck of his life in hitting all the sound spots in getting across. But I wouldn't follow him for a thousand dollars a minute!"

The mad hotel man was soon lost to view on the other side of one of the little hills of sand.

There would have been little sense in trying to follow him or to head him off, even by more roundabout courses. Ashby was now far enough away to elude any pursuit that might start.

"I wonder if Reade has any idea of what he's up against now?" murmured the mayor of Paloma. "That crazy man is loose, and sooner or later he'll be heard from again."

CHAPTER XX. DUFF PROMISES THE "SQUARE DEAL"

Altogether the day had been a hugely satisfactory one to the young chief engineer.

The first test had been made, and, all had passed off well, for, in Tom Reade's easy-going, fearless mind the peculiar doings of George Ashby did not figure at all as a part of the day's work.

"Harry, we've every reason to feel proud of ourselves" mused Tom aloud, as he undressed in the shack that night.

"You feel pretty certain that we've conquered the Man-killer, do you?" Hazelton asked, as he laid down the book he had been reading.

Of late, since the burning of the Cactus House, the chums had slept in the shack, though still getting many of their meals in town.

"Oh, of course you know that we haven't won, the whole fight yet," Reade went on. "We've plenty of work to do here still before we pronounce the job finished. But to-day's shows that our plan for filling in this particular, kind of quicksand was a sound one. You know the president of the road said that words failed to express his complete approbation of our work."

"We certainly have been remarkably fortunate—so far," Harry admitted. "Yet I must confess, Tom, that I'm still nervous."

"Then it must be over Ashby," Tom laughed.

"Ashby be hanged!" Hazelton retorted. "I haven't given him a thought this evening. No, I'm still nervous about our job here. The first test was all right— that is, it was all right to-day. But these quicksands are treacherous. Our roadbed may be all right for a fortnight, and may seem as safe as we could wish it to be. Then, all of a sudden, within sixty seconds, it may sink before our very eyes. Suppose it were to sink while a trainload of human beings was passing over it!"

"You might as well dismiss all such thoughts," Reade counseled. "I tell you, Harry, we've proved that our principle is sound. Now, we will go ahead and finish the job. When we go away from here I, for one, shall feel certain that the Man-killer must behave for all time to come. Harry, there's a limit to the shifting tendency of a quicksand, and to-day's test proves to me that we've found it. We've won. I wish I were as sure of a dozen other things as I am that we've won out here to-day."

"All right, then," smiled Hazelton. "You're a smarter engineer than I am, Tom, old fellow. If you're satisfied, then I'm bound to be, for I'll back your judgment in engineering against my own."

"That's rather more praise, Harry, than I expect or wish," Reade rejoined soberly. "But I don't see how the Man-killer can ever again assert himself against the A. G. & N. M.'s roadbed."

"Oh, I'm only an old croaker, I know," Harry confessed. "I've got a blue streak on to-night. Or else it's a fit of apprehension about something or other. I feel as if—"

Crack! crack!

Outside two shots rang suddenly out, to be followed by a dozen swift, scattering reports.

"Mr. Reade! They—" began a voice outside, then stopped abruptly.

Tom hustled on his clothing again with a speed that seemed to partake of magic. Then, with Harry close upon his heels, he rushed to the door, jerking it open.

"Just the pair we want!" snarled a voice that proceeded from behind a mask.

A dozen masked men pressed into the room. Tom and Harry put their fists into instant action, but it availed them nothing.

In a twinkling they were borne to the floor. At lightning speed both were rolled over and bound.

From the tents of the laborers, beyond hoarse voices sounded as the men were awakened by the shots.

"Get back there, you idiots!" commanded a voice outside. "If you don't, you'll think that a Gatling gun factory has blown up about your ears."

Reports rang out sharply as a dozen revolver shots were fired into the air.

Now, dazed with the suddenness of the attack, Reade and Hazelton were dragged into the open.

Their two night watchmen, who had gone down bravely, now lay wounded on the ground, their weapons snatched from them.

"Hoist 'em along, boys," ordered a gruff voice.

Tom and Harry were carried on the shoulders of men, and moved along at a swift pace. Only half a dozen of the raiders needed to remain somewhat in the rear, firing an occasional shot to prevent the unarmed laborers from swarming to the attack.

"Hoist 'em up! Tie 'em on! Get under way quick! There'll be a big noise raised after us soon," declared the same directing voice.

Tom and Harry were fairly thrown upon the backs of horses, and there lashed fast.

"Mount and get away," ordered the commander of this strangest of night raids.

Two men, each leading a pony to which a captive was lashed, rode off in one direction. Groups of two or three rode away in other directions, the blackness of the night swallowing them up.

It was going to be a difficult task for pursuers to know which direction to take in order to come up with Reade and Hazelton in time to save them from the fate that lay just ahead of them!

For audacity and dash the raid could not have been better planned.

From camp not a shot was fired, for the watchmen had had the only weapons and these had been seized by the invaders.

"Our foremen might telegraph to camp," thought Tom swiftly, as he felt himself being carried away. "But I'll wager that these smart scoundrels didn't forget to cut the wire before springing the raid."

For the first two or three minutes Harry's, slower moving mind hardly grasped more than the fact that their enemies appeared to have won a complete triumph.

"There isn't much doubt as to what they'll do with us," thought Hazelton, with a slight shudder. "These rascals will move too fast for pursuit to overtake them early. What they in intend to do with us can be done in a very few minutes."

Neither young engineer really expected to live to see daylight. From the first, after having incurred the anger of a certain lawless element in Paloma, the young engineers had understood fully that threats of lynching them had not been idly made.

"There'll be a stir, though," Tom Reade muttered to himself. "The A. G. & N. M. officials won't let this crime go by without a determined effort to bring the offenders to justice. Detectives will search this community in squads, and everyone of these masked gentlemen is likely to get his deserts."

Within the next half hour the galloping horses had covered fully five miles. Now the leader of the crowd led the way down into a deep gully in the sand.

"Hold up, men," ordered the leader, and the cavalcade came to a stop, horses panting.

"Tumble the cattle off into the dirt," was the next order, and it was obeyed, Tom and Harry rolling in the bitter alkali dust.

"Now, gentlemen, I believe I will take command," spoke one of the party of horsemen, in his most suave voice, as he removed his mask. The speaker, as Reade knew at once, was Jim Duff, the gambler.

"That's all right, Jim," nodded the former leader.

"Jake, ride back a few hundred yards and keep a sharp lookout," suggested Duff blandly. "The pursuers may come in automobiles. We'll cut the ceremonies here short and leave nothing but lifeless bodies for the rescue parties to find."

Stakes were driven and the horses picketed.

"Bring along our guests," suggested Jim Duff, with a touch of humor that the occasion rendered grisly.

Thereupon Tom and Harry were once more jerked to their feet.

"Ye can walk, I reckon, and don't have be toted," observed one of the scoundrels.

"We're wholly at your service, sir," rejoined Tom mockingly.

"And equally at your pleasure," Harry suggested dryly.

Two hundred yards further on the halted close to a pair of stunted trees of about the same size.

"Gentlemen, you may as well remove your masks on this hot evening," suggested Jim Duff. The face coverings came off. Reade and Hazelton surveyed their captors as the chance offered, being careful not to betray too great curiosity.

"I see one gentleman here whom I had expected to find," remarked Tom quietly.

"Me?" hinted Duff.

"Well, yes; you, for one, but I refer to that excellent host, Mr. Ashby, of the Mansion House."

With a start George Ashby turned on Reade, coming closer and grinning ferociously into the face of the young chief engineer. Tom, however, managed to muster a smile as he went on:

"How do you do, Mr. Ashby? Your performance of this afternoon mystified me a good deal. I had never expected to find myself on a shooting acquaintance with you."

Three or four of the rascals chuckled at this way of putting it, but Proprietor Ashby snarled like a wild animal.

"As for you, Mr. Duff," Reade resumed, "I confess that I have never been able to understand you."

"You will to-night," smiled Duff, with bland ferocity. "I can promise you, as a gambler, that I am going to give you a square deal."

"Fine!" glowed Tom. "I am delighted to hear that you have reformed, then."

This' time there was a general laugh. Jim Duff flushed angrily.

"Reade, what you never understood about me is that I belong to the ranks of the square gamblers."

"I didn't believe there were any such gamblers," Tom replied in a voice of surprise. "It is still hard for me to believe. How can any man be square and honorable when he won't work, but fattens on the earnings of others? Has that idea any connection with honor?"

"Stop that line of talk, you young hound!" ordered Duff, striding up to this bold young enemy. All the slight veneer of polish that Duff usually affected had vanished now. His eyes blazed with rage as he doubled his fist and struck Reade full in the face, knocking him down. One of the bystanders jerked Tom to his feet.

"Speaking of the square deal," Tom observed, "I now insist upon it. Duff, you knocked me down when my hands were tied. If you're not a coward I request that you order my hands freed—and then repeat your blow if you dare."

"You'll stay tied," retorted Duff grimly.

"I knew it," sighed Reade. "What's the use of talking about honor and square dealing where a gambler is concerned? Loaded dice, marked cards or tying a man before you dare to hit him—it's all the same to your kind."

"Shut up that talk, you hound, or I'll pound you stiff before we go on with what's been arranged for you!" raged the gambler, shaking his clenched fist in the face of the young engineer.

"Go slowly, Jim," advised one of the men present. "Of course we know what we're to do to this young pup, and we all know what he thinks of you. But some of the rest of us have different ideas as to how a helpless enemy ought to be treated."

"You, Rafe Bodson!" snarled Duff, turning on the last speaker. "Are you one of us? Do you belong to our side, or are you a spy for the other crowd?"

"Got your gun with you, Duff?" inquired Bodson calmly.

"Yes," snapped the gambler.

"Get it out in your hand, then, before you talk to me any more in that fashion."

"He won't," mocked Tom. "He doesn't dare, Bodson. Your hands are not tied."

"Cut it out, Rafe! Quit it!" ordered one of the other men in the crowd. "We won't let this tenderfoot split our ranks. You're one of us, and you'll stand by us."

"Not if there's going to be any more hitting of tied men," retorted Bodson sulkily. "There's a limit to what a man can stand."

"Thank you, my friend," broke in Tom Reade mildly. "But don't go to any trouble on our account. There are few if any others in this crowd who can understand the meaning of fair play—the gambler least of all."

"I'll take that out of you, Reade!" blazed Jim Duff. "I'll—"

"You'll do nothing while the kid's hands are tied," objected Bodson, stepping between the pair. "Act fair and square, Jim, as a man should act."

"That's the argument, Rafe," remarked another man, also stepping forward.

"Bully for you, Jeff Moore," replied Rafe. "Now, remember, friends, we're not calling for anything except that Jim Duff live up to the program he just published for himself—the square deal."

Several murmurs of protest came from the other raiders.

"I reckon, Rafe, you and Jeff had better step back and let the rest of us handle this thing," advised one of the party. "The pair of you are too chicken-livered for us."

"It's a lie, as anyone in Paloma knows," Rafe retorted coolly. "No—put up your shooters," as the hands of five or six men slid to their belts. "There's no need of bad blood between us. All I ask is for Jim Duff to step back out of this."

"Am I the leader here or am I not?" demanded Duff boldly. "Wasn't it my interests that were first assailed by these fresh tenderfeet! Didn't you gentlemen come out to-night, to help me attend to my affair? Didn't you turn also to avenge the blow that has been dealt these cubs to poor George Ashby's prosperity?"

At hearing himself so sympathetically referred to, Ashby threw himself forward, a short, double-barreled shotgun in his hands.

"Yes, you, get back, you white-livered cowards!" commanded Ashby hoarsely. "You let Duff and myself and the rest of us here handle these young hounds as they deserve to be treated. You, Rafe and Jeff, get out of this. You've no business here. You belong to the enemies of business interests in Paloma. The rest of us will settle with these business destroyers."

Ashby's eyes glowed with the unbridled fury of the lunatic. Yet Rafe Bodson did not waver.

"Gentlemen," he demanded coldly, "for what purpose did you bring these young fellows out here?"

"To lynch 'em!" came the hoarse murmur.

"Then go ahead and do it, like men," ordered Bodson. "There are the trees. You have your ropes, and your men are ready. Remember, no cowardly treatment of young fellows whose hands are tied. Go on with the lynching and get it over with!"

CHAPTER XXI. A SPECIALIST IN "HONOR"

"Sir! Stop it, I tell you," quivered Duff, again stepping to the front. "These young hounds shan't die until I've made them apologize for every insulting word they've said to me."

"Fine!" glowed Tom with enthusiasm.

"Great!"

"What ails you now, Reade?" demanded Duff, his face again darkening.

"You've just promised us that we shall live forever," returned Tom dryly.

Then he added, with a sigh:

"But I suppose that's only another lie—another specimen of a gambler's honor."

"Stand aside, Bodson! Moore, you get out of the way!" snarled the gambler, his anger again depriving him of all reason. "I'll have my way with these young hounds before we string 'em up."

"Let me at 'em!" implored Ashby, fingering his shotgun nervously. "Get out of my way. I don't want to pepper anyone else."

But Bodson and Moore, bad as they were some respects, stood their ground.

"Are you going to let us at them?" insisted Duff, his voice now broken and harsh from anger.

"Not for the purpose of bullying them!" insisted Rafe, without moving. "Jeff, you're with me, aren't you?"

"Right by your side, pardner."

"Come on, then, boys!" called Duff, the note of rally in his tone. "Help me to drive this pair of traitors out of your company."

Like a flash Bodson's revolver was in his band. The muzzle covered the gambler.

"Jim Duff, down on your knees before I blow your bead off!"

The gambler started back, his face paling.

In the same instant Jeff Moore had also drawn his revolver, and held it ready for the first hostile sign from anyone in the group.

"What's the matter with you, Rafe?" demanded the gambler, in a half-coaxing tone.

"Nothing," Bodson assured him calmly, "except that I'm going to blow your head off if you aren't down on your knees before I've counted three! One— two—th—"

Duff dropped to his knees, holding his hands high in air.

"Now apologize for calling us traitors," admonished Rafe. "Do it handsomely, too, while you're about it."

"Rafe," protested Jim Duff, "you, know that I said what I did only because I was angry. I know you're a gentleman, and you know that I know it. If I've hurt your feelings, I'm sorry, a thousand times over."

"Jim, you're a good deal of a sneak, aren't you?" inquired Rafe, in a voice that sounded pleasant enough, but which carried a warning in its tone.

"Yes," Duff admitted. "I guess I'm a good deal of a sneak."

"Get up on your feet, then. We understand one another," said Bodson. "Go ahead, if you want to, and carry out your plans for a merry evening. But don't make the mistake of calling ugly names again, and don't forget all you've said about the square deal. Hang these tenderfeet, if that's what you want to do, but don't hit men without first giving them a chance to hit back."

Duff, shaking partly from fear, though more from a sense of his humiliation, rose to his feet. For a moment he stood choking down his varied emotions. Then, with an attempt at his old-time, suave banter, he inquired:

"Are you young gentlemen ready for the collar and neck-tie party that we've planned to give you?"

"As ready as you are," observed Tom dryly.

"And you?" asked Duff, turning to Hazelton. "Are you ready?"

"I'm not particular about feeling a lariat around my neck," Harry answered, "but I'll follow my friend Reade anywhere—even where you propose to send us."

"Ay, but that's courage of the kind you don't expect to find in a blamed tenderfoot!" remarked Jeff Moore, resting a hand first on Tom's shoulder and then on Harry's.

"Why?" asked Tom. "Does it surprise you?"

"It shore does," replied Jeff.

"Is courage a matter of geography, then?" Tom inquired.

"I—I—pardner, you've got me there," Jeff admitted, looking puzzled. "Yet, somehow, I never looked for much courage in a fellow who hailed from east of the Mississippi."

George Ashby had been looking on during the last few moments, his eyes glittering strangely. Yet, as he said nothing, the attention of the others had turned from him.

Jeff Moore happened to turn just in time to see the muzzle of the shotgun turned fully on Tom Reade's waist line, and Ashby's forefinger resting on one of the triggers.

Bang! spoke the gun, a sheet of flame leaped forth.

Tom Reade did not even start. All his nerve had come to the surface in that instant. He was unharmed, for Jeff's sweeping arm had knocked aside the muzzle of the gun and the shot had entered the leg of one of the raiders.

"What'd you do that for, Jeff?" groaned the injured man, sinking to the alkali dust.

But Moore was busy with the mad hotel keeper, having clinched with him, and now being engaged in taking away the shotgun, one barrel of which was still loaded.

"Stand back there, friends," warned Rafe Bodson, who still held his revolver in his right hand. "We don't want to see any more of the party hurt."

Jeff had the gun in a moment, despite the insane fury with which Ashby fought.

"Take care of this, Rafe," requested Jeff, turning over the gun, which Bodson received with his left hand.

Ashby, momentarily free, sprang at the new bolder of the weapon, but Moore tripped him and fell upon him.

The other men stood by as though fascinated, not interfering. Perhaps they felt that their safety depended upon Ashby's being disarmed.

There was a short, sharp scuffle on the ground after which Moore rose, leaving the hotel man with his hands tied behind his back.

"And I request," remarked Moore, "that no gentleman present cut the knots that I have tied. It'll be a favor to me to have Ashby left alone for the present."

"Now, then, Rafe or Jeff," spoke the gambler, mustering up what remained of his courage, "since you two have taken charge of affairs, won't you be good enough to inform us what your pleasure is?"

"We're not in charge," retorted Bodson sullenly. "All we've undertaken to do is to look out for the square deal that you promised, Duff, and which you didn't exhibit in a way that we liked. As for the rest, go ahead when you like—but don't do any more hitting with your fists."

"We'll go ahead with the lariat, then?" hinted Duff eagerly.

"If that's the pleasure of the gentlemen," Bodson agreed, bowing slightly.

To the gambler it seemed the opportune moment to rush matters.

"Bring up lariats, two of you," Duff ordered, turning around to the others. "And don't waste time over it."

The rawhide ropes were brought. The gambler himself tied the nooses, testing them to see that they ran freely.

"Bring Reade and Hazelton under the trees," was Duff's next order, which was obeyed. Bodson and Moore, their weapons still in their hands, followed, keeping keen watch over the way the affair was conducted.

"Any choice of trees Reade?" inquired Jin Duff.

"None," answered Tom shortly. His face was pallid and set, though he did not show any other sign of fear.

"Hazelton?"

"One tree is as good as another," Harry answered in a strangely quiet voice.

In the midst of an impressive silence, and with motions that seemed oddly unreal to the tended victims, Duff placed the two young engineers. A lariat was thrown over a low limb of each of the trees. Then, with slightly trembling hands the gambler adjusted a over the neck of each bound boy.

CHAPTER XXII. TOM AND HARRY VANISH

"How d'ye like that, Rafe?" queried Jeff Moore, as Jim Duff stepped back and viewed the young engineers with a diabolical smile before giving the fatal signal.

"I don't like it," muttered Bodson.

"No more do I."

"Shall we stop it?"

"Yes. I'm sick of Jim Duff. This night has turned me against the smooth-tongued coward."

"Get busy, then, Rafe!"

"Shall we stand the crowd off and set the boys free?"

"Pump both of your shooting-irons loose into the air—I'll do the rest," replied Moore.

Cr-r-r-rack! Pointing his weapons skyward, Bodson had quickly obeyed Moore's command.

"Now, what—" began one of the raiders, wheeling instantly.

"Rafe's going to give 'em a proper send off," grinned one of Duff's men.

"No!" shouted the other. "That's a bluff. He and Jeff are trying to queer the whole game."

With cries of anger, several of the men sprang toward Jeff, who had bared his sheath knife and was about to free Tom and Harry.

"Here—stop that, you traitors!" roared Duff, leaping forward.

"I've four shots left, Jim," remarked Rafe Bodson calmly, as he ceased firing. "Call me names, if you think it wise."

Like a flash Duff drew one of his own revolvers. Before he had time to fire, however, three men threw themselves between Bodson and the gambler.

"Stop talking gun play, Rafe," warned one of the three. "Act like a gentleman."

"I've forgotten how to do that," Rafe remarked. "I've traveled with this outfit too long."

"Put up your guns. Then we'll attend to this pair of youngsters."

"My guns remain in my hands," Bodson declared coolly. "I expect to die with my boots on to-night. I reckon Jeff has figured it out the same way."

"I have," Moore answered coolly, as he stepped over beside Bodson. Then deliberately, yet with an indescribably swift motion, he drew two revolvers.

"Stand out, Jim Duff! Be a man, for once in your miserable career," ordered Rafe Bodson. "Don't try to protect yourself by hiding behind the bodies of men who don't know any better than to follow your lead."

Jim Duff didn't accept the challenge. Instead, he crouched behind two of his followers, taking deliberate aim with his revolver at Bodson.

But he never fired that cowardly shot. Like a flash from the sky came an interruption that created panic among the assembled scoundrels.

"Here we have 'em, gentlemen," announced the steady voice of Superintendent Hawkins from the western end of the gully. "Get 'em all rounded up. If they've done Mr. Reade and Mr. Hazelton any injury then don't let one of them get away alive."

The low sand piles near by seemed swarming with men. The steel barrels of firearms glistened even in the darkness.

The scout had been sent out to the eastward. None had thought of watching the western approach to the gully.

"Shoot, boys!" screamed Jim Duff, wheeling in a sudden frenzy of desperation. He fired straight in the direction of Hawkins's voice.

In another instant the air was rent with the sound of shots. Flashes from many revolvers lit up the darkness almost as well as torches could have done.

Jim Duff, having started his followers to firing, stole off in the darkness, leaving them to bear the brunt of the return fire of Hawkins and his men.

George Ashby lay on the ground bound as he had been left, his sawed-off shotgun not far away and his belt full of shells.

"Rouse yourself, Ash!" muttered the gambler, as he slashed the hotel man's bonds with his knife. "Get your gun, but don't use it now. Move quickly, and we'll get away from here and take Reade and Hazelton with us. Put your mind on your work, Ash, and follow my orders. Don't try to think too much for yourself. Here, this way!"

The scene of the fighting had already shifted from the immediate neighborhood of the twin trees. Duff guided his mad companion along in the darkness until they halted close to where the two engineers stood bound, powerless to join in the fray.

"Shall we shoot them here and now?" whispered Ashby, a wild light glittering in his eyes.

"No," returned Duff. "We'll sneak up behind them, club them with revolvers and carry, them off. Then we can do as we please with them. You quiet Hazelton and I'll attend to Reade."

The two scoundrels crept up behind their victims.

A moment later Duff quickly cut the lariat about the neck of Tom Reade, who had been rendered unconscious from the terrific blow dealt him by the gambler. Ashby had been equally successful in "quieting" Hazelton.

"Now hustle," ordered Duff. "You pick up Hazelton. I'll take Reade. Carry 'em over your shoulder—that's the way to do. Now, follow me and don't make a sound. We'll please ourselves this night with what we'll do to the meddling pair!"

With Tom Reade over his shoulder, senseless and inert, Duff started off in the darkness, while the rattle of firearms continued.

George Ashby, muttering to himself, followed with Harry Hazelton.

The gambler staggered slightly under the weight of his human burden. Yet he moved rapidly, a strange eagerness lighting up his eyes.

Jim Duff knew that he would never again dare to enter the town of Paloma, yet the gambler thirsted, before fleeing to new scenes, to be revenged on Tom Reade. With that object in view, Duff was willing to take great risks.

As for Ashby, who, still clutching his shotgun in his left hand, staggered along under the burden of Hazelton's weight, the hotel man was no longer responsible for his actions. Rage and wickedness had made him a maniac, who might be restrained but could not be punished by law.

Within two minutes the firing behind them died out. Soon there were distant sounds of searching. Plainly Hawkins and the other friends of the young engineers were hunting diligently for Tom and Harry.

"Dump your man, Ashby," commanded Jim Duff, halting at last. "It will be a mistake to go too far. Their friends won't expect to find 'em so close, and they'll soon be searching farther away."

So Ashby dropped Harry on to the sand beside Tom. Then the wickedest possible gleam came into the hotel man's eyes as he loaded his shotgun.

"We'll fill 'em full of lead right here and now," whispered the hotel keeper. "Then we'll be sure that they can't get away from us again."

"Not so fast!" retorted Duff warningly. "We can't shoot now. If we do, there'll be no way to get out of this alive. Look yonder!"

Duff swung his mad friend around, pointing to a gleam of light that shone out over the desert.

"An automobile," muttered the gambler. "And there's another—and another! There must be six or eight of them out to-night, and all of 'em crammed with fighting men. A shot would bring two or three carloads of ugly fellows down upon us."

"What are we going to do, then?" demanded the hotel keeper, in a menacing tone.

"Wait awhile," urged the gambler. "You're seeing what the plan of the enemy is. They're circling about, but they're further out from the gully than we are. The cars will go on cutting larger and larger circle, and all the time getting farther away from us. In half an hour the cars and the men will be so far away that we need give no thought to them. Then we can attend to Reade and Hazelton."

"What are you going to do with them?" demanded Ashby in a whisper, his cunning eyes lighting with a fire of added eagerness.

"We'll get 'em awake, first of all," nodded Jim Duff. "Then we'll attend to them."

"Remember, they ruined my business!" whispered the hotel man.

"Well, didn't they ruin my business, too?" snarled Duff. "Didn't they cant like a pair of hypocrites, and turn hundreds of their workmen against coming in to play in my place? Didn't these young hounds keep me from winning thousands of dollars of railroad money? Ash, I tell you, these young fellows have hit me hard! First, they broke up my games. Next, they talked their men out of going into Paloma and spending money for drink. Why, Ash, next thing you know, they would have brought missionaries to Paloma to convert men and to build churches!"

As Ashby glared at the unconscious boys from under his black brows he looked as though he believed them capable of all the wickedness that Jim Duff's imagination had charged against them.

"I can't wait!" groaned the hotel man. "Just one barrel of shot apiece into each of 'em!"

"No, no, no, Ash! Haven't I always been your good friend?"

"You surely have, Jim Duff," admitted the mad hotel man. "You're the one man alive to-night that I'd trust."

"Then trust me a little further," coaxed the gambler virtuously. "Trust to my brains tonight, George, and you'll feast on revenge!"

"But you keep me waiting so long for it!" complained the lunatic.

"Don't you trust me, George?"

"You know I do, Jim Duff."

"Then trust me a little longer. Be quiet, and be patient."

"But—"

"Sh!" warned Duff suddenly, throwing himself flat on the ground. "Down with you, Ash!"

"What is it?" whispered the hotel man in the gambler's ear as he too sank to the ground.

"Sh!" once more warned the gambler. "Use your eyes, George. Look out over the sand in the darkness. Do you see two men prowling this way?"

"Yes," assented the hotel man, after a pause.

"They're looking for us—enemies, George. Use all your cunning. Above all, be silent and lie low! Don't make a move, unless I tell you to do so. Show your trust in me, Ash, as you've never shown it before. If you don't, we'll be cheated out of our revenge!"

CHAPTER XXIII. RAFE AND JEFF MISCALCULATE

The two men whom the craven gambler had sighted were coming slowly onward, their movements suggesting a good deal of care and watchfulness.

Nor did they come in a wholly straight line. That they did not suspect the nearness of Jim Duff and his mad companion was plain at a glance.

"Burrow in the sand!" whispered the gambler in Ashby's ear. "Quiet! Be ready, but don't do anything unless I give you the word."

"When you do give me the word," trembled the hotel man, "I'll kill 'em both."

"Not unless we have to do so—remember!" ordered the gambler. "We want, if possible, to take 'em alive."

Let us now go back to the two men whom Duff and Ashby were watching so closely.

They were Rafe Bodson and Jeff Moore.

Both had come out of the recent fighting unharmed. Neither Rafe nor Jeff had fired a shot at the invading forces led by Hawkins. Instead, the pair had slipped stealthily away, until they had gotten out of the immediate zone of the hot firing. Then they hid under some bushes.

"An hour ago I'd have felt like a sneak, not standing by the gang any better," whispered Jeff uneasily.

"Same here," Rafe admitted. "In fact, I'm wondering whether I acted straight in running off like this."

"Aren't you sure about it in your own mind?" asked Jeff slowly.

"Almost," Rafe returned. "All that bothers me is not sticking by the same crowd that we started out with to-night. As for Jim Duff—"

"He's poison, and deadly poison at that," broke in Jeff.

"That's just what he is, pardner."

"Yet I used to like Duff pretty well."

"So did I," nodded Jeff. "But that was when I thought he had some sand."

"The fellow's a skulking coyote!"

"A coyote is brave, compared with Jim Duff," contended Jeff Moore.

"Reade and Hazelton showed the real sand!"

"I never thought tenderfeet could be as brave," glowed Moore.

"Jeff, I reckon Reade and Hazelton aren't real tenderfeet any more. They've been west some time. But, then, such fellows wouldn't be tenderfeet even if they lived in New Jersey all the time. Courage belongs in some fellows, no matter where they work."

"The fighting seems to be over," observed Jeff Moore.

"Then the friends of the two engineers must have found them," suggested Bodson.

"It doesn't sound like it over there. The newcomers seem to be doing a lot of hunting in the gully."

"Let's move in closer," proposed Rafe.

Crawling on their stomachs, the pair moved in closer. As they arrived, unseen, they were in time to see the late fighting men clamber into their automobiles. Hawkins could be heard giving directions for the further search for Reade and Hazelton.

Then the cars started away.

"What do you reckon?" demanded Jeff, looking at Bodson.

"I reckon some of Duff's crowd slipped out of the fight, got the two youngsters, and slipped away with them," Bodson answered.

"Then it was Duff—he was one of 'em," returned Jeff, with a strong conviction. "From what I've seen of Duff to-night he'd rather do a running trick than a fighting one."

"It would take two to carry both youngsters away. Who was the other one?" Rafe wondered aloud.

"Most likely the fellow who'd mind Duff best."

"That must mean poor George Ashby."

"Let's slip into the gully and see what we can find."

One fact learned in the gully astonished both investigators. Despite the volleys that had been fired no dead or wounded men lay about. Of course Hawkins could have taken any injured men away in the automobiles. Plainly the raiders had been equally fortunate in getting their wounded away on their horses. Mounted men familiar with the desert would know many paths where horses could travel, but where automobiles could not follow.

"Our hosses are gone," discovered Jeff a few moments.

"Of course," nodded Rafe. "The crowd we were out with wouldn't be slow in a simple little piece of every-day honesty like stealing hosses!"

"I'm through with any such gang after this, Rafe. How about you?"

"I'm shore going to be careful about the kind of company I pick. But, Jeff, we'll have to travel away from these parts. No good company around here would welcome us. They wouldn't like the only references we could give, Jeff."

"Oh, shore, we'll have to travel," agreed Moore. "That is, if the sheriff doesn't take up our tickets before we get started."

"All this talk isn't showing us what became of Reade and Hazelton," remarked Rafe Bodson. "Let's go back under the trees and see if we can find what has become of Reade and Hazelton. Before I change my post-office box I'm going to try to do those two youngsters a good turn."

So the pair had started off. Yet, like the automobile searchers, Jeff and Rafe did not expect to run across Tom and Harry and their captors so close to the gully.

For this reason the pair proceeded without very much caution at the outset.

Even now, after Duff and Ashby had sighted them, Moore and Bodson halted twice to light matches and examine the trail that their keen eyes had discovered as moving westward from the gully.

"Now, I reckon we've got the general direction," muttered Rafe Bodson when, after having once more discovered the tracks he turned and got the general course. "We know the way to head."

"Then we won't light any more matches," suggested Jeff. "It might get us into trouble."

Accordingly they kept on, guiding themselves now by their general knowledge of the country.

Jim Duff and Ashby were well concealed, not only by the sand, but by a little fringe of brush as well.

Hence it is not to be wondered at that Bodson and Moore went forward to be astonished by a sudden movement in the sand, followed by a hail of "Gentlemen, get your hands up, or take your medicine!"

The command came in Jim Duff's tones.

He was barely thirty feet away from the surprised pair, one of his revolvers leveled so to drop Bodson at a touch of the trigger.

George Ashby's sawed-off shotgun looked squarely at the region bounded by Jeff Moore's belt.

"It's your turn, gentlemen," agreed Rafe, he put his hands in the air.

"You've got us—be decent," grinned Jeff, as he, too, raised his hands upward.

"Get your hands up higher!" ordered Jim Duff in his deadliest tone. These men were now helpless, and the gambler merely chuckled inwardly at the thought.

"Is this where we shoot them?" queried the mad hotel keeper.

"Yes—after a minute or two!" nodded Jim Duff, who wished first to determine whether the automobiles of the searching party were moving too near to them.

"I can hardly wait for the word!" quivered Ashby.

CHAPTER XXIV. CONCLUSION

"How long are we to keep our hands up, Duff?" questioned Jeff.

"Quiet," hissed the gambler. "I'm listening."

"If it's for friends of ours," grimaced Rafe Bodson, "you needn't listen any longer. We haven't any friends in either crowd now."

"Quiet, I tell you!" snarled Duff.

No noise of moving automobiles came to the gambler's keen ears in the darkness of the night.

"Ready," faintly whispered Duff, giving Ashby a slight nudge.

"Shoot 'em?" whispered the mad hotel man.

"Yes; you hit Jeff. I'll take care of Rafe!"

Just then darkness fell upon the gambler. He was knocked flat and senseless by a blow of a fist from behind.

In the same instant a man leaped upon George Ashby, bearing him to earth.

Bang! The noise of the discharging shotgun broke on the night's stillness. Bang! crashed the other barrel.

The muzzle had been pointed skyward, however, and both charges of buckshot had been driven off into space, to fall to the earth many yards beyond.

"Reade! Hazelton!" choked Rafe Bodson, leaping forward. "You fellows certainly have grit! Here, Hazelton, let me help you with that loco (crazy) hotel man."

Jeff, in the meantime had rolled Jim Duff over on his back, then sat on him. When Duff returned to consciousness he found himself gazing into the muzzle of an automatic revolver.

Harry and Bodson made a quick, sure job of tying Ashby's wrists with a cord that Rafe supplied.

"You think you've stopped me, don't you?" snarled the hotel man, wild with rage.

"We stopped you in time to keep you from shooting down two men who were at your mercy," retorted Harry sternly.

"What's that?" gasped Rafe.

"They were going to shoot you with your hands in the air," Tom declared.

"That's another of your lies, Reade," snarled the gambler.

"It's you who are doing the lying, Duff," rejoined Tom stiffly. "I came to my senses just in time to hear you tell Ashby to kill one man while you killed the other."

"So that was the game, was it?" said Jeff.

"No, it wasn't," snapped Jim Duff.

"Shut up," ordered Jeff unbelievingly. "Duff, we've seen enough of you to-night to know that an Apache has ten times as much honor as you have, and a rattlesnake has twenty times as much decency. You lying, miserable, white-livered, smooth-tongued, poisonous reptile in human form. If you open your mouth to say another word you'll have me so wild that I'll pull the trigger of this automatic before I intend to do so."

"Thank goodness you had become conscious too, Harry!" breathed Tom fervently. "I don't believe I could have knocked both men over in time to prevent a killing. I managed to get my hands free just in time to get on the job."

"I had known for some moments what was going on around me," Hazelton replied. "But I was lying with my eyes closed, and keeping mighty quiet. I was trying to hear your breathing, so I could decide whether you had come to your senses, when all of a sudden you sat up and freed my hands. Ugh!" he added with disgust, as he reached up and slipped the remnant of rawhide noose from around his neck.

"What'll we do with this snake and, his weak-minded brother?" asked Jeff dryly. "Tie 'em up and ship 'em into Paloma?"

"Fire off your revolver two or three times," suggested Tom, who had caught a faint, far away sound of an automobile. "That may bring a machine over here."

"You shoot, Rafe," urge Moore. "I'll want to keep my weapon handy for this crooked card-sharp."

Rafe obligingly emptied one of his revolvers into the air. From a distance came the honk of an automobile horn, as though in answer to the signal shots. Soon the noise of an automobile engine became more distinct. Finally the body of a large car loomed up in the darkness. A few shouts brought the car to the spot.

"This you, Mr. Reade?" called the joy voice of Superintendent Hawkins. "And Hazelton, safe, also?"

All five seats in this car were occupied. Six more men had to be crowded in somehow, after Jim Duff had been tied with his hands behind him. Most of them had to stand.

"Back to Paloma, as fast as you can go with safety," ordered Mr. Hawkins, as soon as all were inside. "Gracious, but there'll be a joyful demonstration back in camp as soon as the good word is received."

As the car sped along over the desert the story was told of how the pursuit had been made.

It was Mr. Hawkins who had tried to wire from camp into town, calling for cars and posses to go in pursuit of the raiders.

As Tom had imagined at the outset, the raiders had cut the railroad telegraph wire. Discovering this, Mr. Hawkins had leaped on to the bare back of a horse at camp and had covered the distance at a gallop.

Men had been quickly rounded up within the very few minutes that were needed in getting the cars out and ready to run. There were hundreds of men in Paloma who had grown to despise Duff and all the evil crew behind the gambler.

From the outset the leaders of the posse, on hearing, of the direction first taken by the fleeing raiders, had calculated on the gully as the probable place of halting.

While the posse was still on the way out to the gully, and at some distance away, the sound of Ashby's discharging gun had reached them. Reasoning that the raiders would probably place a guard only on the town end of the gully, the posse had made a wide detour, so as to approach the gully from the westward. Leaving the cars at a considerable distance, the pursuers, with Mr. Hawkins at their head, had made quick time on foot.

In the fighting that had followed five men of the posse had been hit, though none dangerously. These wounded men, after the fight, had been sent back to Paloma in one of the automobiles.

"We saw some of the raiders fall during the lighting," said Mr. Hawkins, "but their friends made a quick retreat and got all hands back to their horses. We felt sure they didn't have you, Mr. Reade and Mr. Hazelton, so we let the raiders slip away and spent our time in trying to find where you had been taken or if you had escaped. Well, it's all right now!"

As the automobile party approached the town, searchlights from other cars showed the remaining pursuers had heard the signals sounded by the horn of the first automobile and were returning.

As the returning men entered the outlaying streets the little town was found to be anything but a quiet community. Despite the early morning hour, the streets were crowded.

"Where's the chief of police?" inquired Mr. Hawkins, as the first car entered the town and pulled up.

"I'll find him for you, Cap," offered a man on horseback.

"If you will be so good."

As the horseman galloped away Hawkins signed to the others to step out.

"Duff, we're not going to be troubled with your company much longer," smiled Hawkins.

Tom and Harry had already leaped down to the sidewalk when the gambler was helped to alight. Duff's hands were still behind his back though, unknown to his captors, he had succeeded in working them free.

With a stealthy movement the gambler suddenly reached forward, drawing a revolver from another man's holster.

Ere the owner was aware of the loss of the weapon Duff took full aim at Tom Reade.

Crack!

It was the pistol of a deputy sheriff that spoke first. That officer had been the only one to detect the gambler's action, and he had fired instantly.

Jim Duff sank, to the sidewalk, groaning while the deputy sheriff dryly explained the cause of his firing. A loaded revolver was still gripped in Duff's right hand, though the gambler was too weak and in too much pain to fire.

Dr. Furniss' office was near by, and the young physician, sharing in the popular excitement, was awake. He came out on the run, bending over the wounded man to examine him. "Duff," said Dr. Furniss gravely, after a brief examination, "I deem it my duty to tell you that you've dealt your last card. Have you any wishes to express before we move you?"

"I—want to—talk to—Reade," groaned the injured man.

"Certainly," replied Tom, when the request was repeated to him. Stepping softly to where the gambler lay on the sidewalk, Reade bent over him.

"Duff," said Reade gravely, "you and I haven't always been the best of friends, but I can say honestly that I'm sorry to see you in this plight. I hope that you may recover, yet get some happiness out of life."

But the gambler's eyes blazed with ferocity.

"Don't waste any soft soap on me, Reade," he said slowly, and with many pauses. "The Doc is a fool. I'm going to get well, and there will be just one happiness ahead of me. That will be to find you, wherever you may be, and to what I tried to do to you to-night."

"Can't you forget that sort of thing, Duff?" asked Tom gravely. "Not that I'm afraid of you; you've seen enough of me to-night to know that I'm not afraid of you. But I'm afraid for you. You're close to eternity, Duff, and I'd like to see you go to your death with a calm, hopeful, decent mind. I'd like to see you go with a hope of a better life hereafter."

"Don't give me any of your canting talk, Reade," snarled the gambler weakly.

"I'm not going to do so," sighed Tom, rising. "I'm afraid it would be useless. Try to remember, Duff, that I allow myself to have no hard feelings against you. If you possibly can recover I shall be glad to hear that you've done so."

Then Tom stepped over to Dr. Furniss' side, whispering to him:

"Doc, you'll see to it that some clergyman is called, won't you? Any clergyman that is the most likely to reach the heart and the soul of a hardened fellow like Jim Duff."

Dr. Furniss nodded. Men appeared with an old door that was to be used as a stretcher. On this the gambler was placed, and the physician gave him such immediate attention as could be supplied on the sidewalk, for Jim Duff had been shot through the right lung. Then the bearers lifted the door, bearing the gambler back to the now gloomy Mansion House, the doctor following. Ashby, who had been strangely quiet after the shooting, was taken to the local police station and placed in a cell.

Just after the two had been taken care of, and while the crowd still lingered, a young man pushed his way through to the center of the crowd.

"I heard that Jim Duff had returned to town," began the young man. The speaker was Clarence Farnsworth, the foolish young easterner who had been sadly fleeced by the gambler.

"Yes; Duff came back," said Mr. Hawkins, quietly.

"Where is he?" asked Farnsworth. "I must leave in the morning, and I owe Duff seven hundred dollars. I want to pay it to him."

"Money you lost gambling with Duff?" questioned Hawkins.

"It's a debt of honor that I owe Mr. Duff," Farnsworth replied, flushing considerably.

"Son, take one little hint from me," continued Hawkins. "No money ever lost to a gambler in card playing is a debt of honor. It's merely the liability of a chump and a fool. No gambler ever uses any real honor. Men of honor work for the money that they need or want. Duff had a smooth way of talking, an agreeable manner with his profitable victims, but he never had a shred of honor. It isn't possible to be a gambler and a man of honor. If you've seven hundred dollars that you lost to Duff at cards, put it in your pocket and get out of Paloma as soon as you can. Duff won't need the money, anyway. He's down at the Mansion House, dying of a bullet wound that he got through his last piece of trickery. I hate to speak harshly of a dying man, but I'd like to see you get a grain or two of common sense into your head, boy."

Again Farnsworth flushed, but three or four seasoned Arizona men who stood near by added their advice, in line with that of Mr. Hawkins. Clarence soon edged away.

An hour after daylight Jim Duff died. Dr. Furniss and the others who were with the gambler at the last were unable to state that Duff had offered any expression of regret for his evil life, or for his last wicked acts.

Jim Duff died as he had lived.

George Ashby was sent to an asylum and his property sold for his benefit. After a year he was discharged as cured. He has vanished, swallowed up in some other community, and nothing more has been heard of him.

Trailed by detectives of a fire insurance company, Frank Danes was soon caught and brought back to Arizona. He was fairly convicted of having set the old Cactus House on fire, though he could not be persuaded to admit himself an agent of the Colthwaite Company. Fred Ransom, the other agent, is believed to be still in the employ of the Colthwaite Company's "gloom department."

Mr. Hawkins is still in the employ of the A., G. & N. M. So are foremen Bell, Rivers and Mendoza.

Tim Griggs proved himself so thoroughly while foreman at the building of the new rail-road hotel in Paloma, that he has gone on to other and better work. Griggs is now a prosperous man, and, best of all, he has his little daughter with him.

Lessee Carter has flourished in the new railroad hotel. Rafe Bodson and Jeff Moore are his clerks.

The day came when Tom Reade and Harry Hazelton were able to apply the final and most severe test to the roadbed that ran across the Man-killer quicksand. Their work was finished, and finished splendidly, adding another great triumph to their record as young engineers.

"These hot countries are fine, for a while," grunted Harry Hazelton, as the young engineers left Paloma in a special Pullman car that General Manager Ellsworth had sent for their use.

"They are fine, in fact; but one gets tired of working on a blistering desert. I hope our next long undertaking will be in a country where ice grows as one of the natural fruits."

"Greenland, for instance?" smiled Tom Reade.

"Alaska, at all events," responded Harry hopefully.

"Do you know where I'm figuring on making my next stop?" Tom inquired.

"Whore?"

"In good old Gridley, the town where we were born, boy! I'm fairly aching for a sight of the good old town. Will you go with me?"

"For a few weeks, yes," Harry agreed. "But after that little rest?"

"After our visit to the good old home town," Tom Reade replied, "we'll go anywhere on earth where a good, big chance for engineering offers. Harry, we've yet nearly all of our work ahead of us to do if we're ever going to be real, Class A engineers!"

That our young engineers found still greater work awaiting them will be discovered in the next volume in this series, which is published under the title, "The Young Engineers in Nevada; or, Seeking Fortune on the Turn of a Pick."

In this narrative we find our young friends wholly away from railroad work, but engaged in an even greater undertaking. The adventures awaiting them were more exciting than any they had yet encountered. Fame and fortune, too, offered a greater opportunity. How the young engineers embraced the opportunity will be made plain to our readers.

THE END

CPSIA information can be obtained at www.ICGtesting.com
Printed in the USA
LVOW05s1327160214

373891LV00024B/1026/P